THE
MOON METAL

Garrett P. Serviss

1st WORLD
LIBRARY
Literary Society

The Moon Metal

Garrett P. Serviss

© 1st World Library – Literary Society, 2005
PO Box 2211
Fairfield, IA 52556
www.1stworldlibrary.org
First Edition

LCCN: 2004195620

Softcover ISBN: 1-4218-0441-7
Hardcover ISBN: 1-4218-0341-0
eBook ISBN: 1-4218-0541-3

Purchase *"The Moon Metal"*
as a traditional bound book at:
www.1stWorldLibrary.org/purchase.asp?ISBN=1-4218-0441-7

1st World Library Literary Society is a nonprofit
organization dedicated to promoting literacy by:

- Creating a free internet library accessible from any computer worldwide.
- Hosting writing competitions and offering book publishing scholarships.

The Moon Metal
contributed by Tim, Ed & Rodney
in support of
1st World Library Literary Society

CONTENTS

I

SOUTH POLAR GOLD

When the news came of the discovery of gold at the south pole, nobody suspected that the beginning had been reached of a new era in the world's history. The newsboys cried "Extra!" as they had done a thousand times for murders, battles, fires, and Wall Street panics, but nobody was excited. In fact, the reports at first seemed so exaggerated and improbable that hardly anybody believed a word of them. Who could have been expected to credit a despatch, forwarded by cable from New Zealand, and signed by an unknown name, which contained such a statement as this:

"A seam of gold which can be cut with a knife has been found within ten miles of the south pole."

The discovery of the pole itself had been announced three years before, and several scientific parties were known to be exploring the remarkable continent that surrounds it. But while they had sent home many highly interesting reports, there had been nothing to suggest the possibility of such an amazing discovery as that which was now announced. Accordingly, most sensible people looked upon the New Zealand despatch as a hoax.

But within a week, and from a different source, flashed another despatch which more than confirmed the first. It declared that gold existed near the south pole in practically unlimited quantity. Some geologists said this accounted for the greater depth of the Antarctic Ocean. It had always been noticed that the southern hemisphere appeared to be a little overweighted. People now began to prick up their ears, and many letters of inquiry appeared in the newspapers concerning the wonderful tidings from the south. Some asked for information about the shortest route to the new goldfields.

In a little while several additional reports came, some via New Zealand, others via South America, and all confirming in every respect what had been sent before. Then a New York newspaper sent a swift steamer to the Antarctic, and when this enterprising journal published a four-page cable describing the discoveries in detail, all doubt vanished and the rush began.

Some time I may undertake a description of the wild scenes that occurred when, at last, the inhabitants of the northern hemisphere were convinced that boundless stores of gold existed in the unclaimed and uninhabited wastes surrounding the south pole. But at present I have something more wonderful to relate.

Let me briefly depict the situation.

For many years silver had been absent from the coinage of the world. Its increasing abundance rendered it unsuitable for money, especially when contrasted with gold. The "silver craze," which had raged in the closing decade of the nineteenth century, was already a forgotten incident of financial history.

The gold standard had become universal, and business all over the earth had adjusted itself to that condition. The wheels of industry ran smoothly, and there seemed to be no possibility of any disturbance or interruption. The common monetary system prevailing in every land fostered trade and facilitated the exchange of products. Travellers never had to bother their heads about the currency of money; any coin that passed in New York would pass for its face value in London, Paris, Berlin, Rome, Madrid, St. Petersburg, Constantinople, Cairo, Khartoum, Jerusalem, Peking, or Yeddo. It was indeed the "Golden Age," and the world had never been so free from financial storms.

Upon this peaceful scene the south polar gold discoveries burst like an unheralded tempest.

I happened to be in the company of a famous bank president when the confirmation of those discoveries suddenly filled the streets with yelling newsboys. "Get me one of those 'extras'!" he said, and an office-boy ran out to obey him. As he perused the sheet his face darkened.

"I'm afraid it's too true," he said, at length. "Yes, there seems to be no getting around it. Gold is going to be as plentiful as iron. If there were not such a flood of it, we might manage, but when they begin to make trousers buttons out of the same metal that is now locked and guarded in steel vaults, where will be our standard of worth? My dear fellow," he continued, impulsively laying his hand on my arm, "I would as willingly face the end of the world as this that's coming!"

"You think it so bad, then?" I asked. "But most people will not agree with you. They will regard it as very good news."

"How can it be good?" he burst out. "What have we got to take the place of gold? Can we go back to the age of barter? Can we substitute cattle-pens and wheat-bins for the strong boxes of the Treasury? Can commerce exist with no common measure of exchange?"

"It does indeed look serious," I assented.

"Serious! I tell you, it is the deluge!"

Thereat he clapped on his hat and hurried across the street to the office of another celebrated banker.

His premonitions of disaster turned out to be but too well grounded. The deposits of gold at the south pole were richer than the wildest reports had represented them. The shipments of the precious metal to America and Europe soon became enormous - so enormous that the metal was no longer precious. The price of gold dropped like a falling stone, with accelerated velocity, and within a year every money centre in the world had been swept by a panic. Gold was more common than iron. Every government was compelled to demonetize it, for when once gold had fallen into contempt it was less valuable in the eyes of the public than stamped paper. For once the world had thoroughly learned the lesson that too much of a good thing is worse than none of it.

Then somebody found a new use for gold by inventing a process by which it could be hardened and tempered, assuming a wonderful toughness and elasticity without losing its non-corrosive property, and in this form it rapidly took the place of steel.

In the mean time every effort was made to bolster up credit. Endless were the attempts to find a substitute for gold. The chemists sought it in their laboratories and the mineralogists in the mountains and deserts. Platinum might have served, but it, too, had become a drug in the market through the discovery of immense deposits. Out of the twenty odd elements which had been rarer and more valuable than gold, such as uranium, gallium, etc., not one was found to answer the purpose. In short, it was evident that since both gold and silver had become too abundant to serve any longer for a money standard, the planet held no metal suitable to take their place.

The entire monetary system of the world must be readjusted, but in the readjustment it was certain to fall to pieces. In fact, it had already fallen to pieces; the only recourse was to paper money, but whether this was based upon agriculture or mining or manufacture, it gave varying standards, not only among the different nations, but in successive years in the same country. Exports and imports practically ceased. Credit was discredited, commerce perished, and the world, at a bound, seemed to have gone back, financially and industrially, to the dark ages.

One final effort was made. A great financial congress was assembled at New York. Representatives of all the nations took part in it. The ablest financiers of Europe and America united the efforts of their genius and the results of their experience to solve the great problem. The various governments all solemnly stipulated to abide by the decision of the congress.

But, after spending months in hard but fruitless labor, that body was no nearer the end of its undertaking than when it first assembled. The entire world awaited its decision with bated breath, and yet the decision was not formed.

At this paralyzing crisis a most unexpected event suddenly opened the way.

II

THE MAGICIAN OF SCIENCE

An attendant entered the room where the perplexed financiers were in session and presented a peculiar-looking card to the president, Mr. Boon. The president took the card in his hand and instantly fell into a brown study. So complete was his absorption that Herr Finster, the celebrated Berlin banker, who had been addressing the chair for the last two hours from the opposite end of the long table, got confused, entirely lost track of his verb, and suddenly dropped into his seat, very red in the face and wearing a most injured expression.

But President Boon paid no attention except to the singular card, which he continued to turn over and over, balancing it on his fingers and holding it now at arm's-length and then near his nose, with one eye squinted as if he were trying to look through a hole in the card.

At length this odd conduct of the presiding officer drew all eyes upon the card, and then everybody shared the interest of Mr. Boon. In shape and size the card was not extraordinary, but it was composed of metal. What metal? That question had immediately arisen in Mr. Boon's mind when the card came into his hand, and now it exercised the wits of all the others. Plainly it was not tin, brass, copper, bronze, silver, aluminum - although its lightness might have suggested that metal - nor even base gold.

The president, although a skilled metallurgist, confessed his inability to say what it was. So intent had he become in examining the curious bit of metal that he forgot it was a visitor's card of introduction, and did not even look for the name which it presumably bore.

As he held the card up to get a better light upon it a stray sunbeam from the window fell across the metal and instantly it bloomed with exquisite colors! The president's chair being in the darker end of the room, the radiant card suffused the atmosphere about him with a faint rose tint, playing with surprising liveliness into alternate canary color and violet.

The effect upon the company of clear-headed financiers was extremely remarkable. The unknown metal appeared to exercise a kind of mesmeric influence, its soft hues blending together in a chromatic harmony which captivated the sense of vision as the ears are charmed by a perfectly rendered song. Gradually all gathered in an eager group around the president's chair.

"What can it be?" was repeated from lip to lip.

"Did you ever see anything like it?" asked Mr. Boon for the twentieth time.

None of them had ever seen the like of it. A spell fell upon the assemblage. For five minutes no one spoke, while Mr. Boon continued to chase the flickering sunbeam with the wonderful card. Suddenly the silence was broken by a voice which had a touch of awe in it:

"It must be the metal!"

The speaker was an English financier, First Lord of the Treasury, Hon. James Hampton-Jones, K.C.B. Immediately everybody echoed his remark, and the strain being thus relieved, the spell dropped from them and several laughed loudly over their momentary aberration.

President Boon recollected himself, and, coloring slightly, placed the card flat on the table, in order more clearly to see the name. In plain red letters it stood forth with such surprising distinctness that Mr. Boon wondered why he had so long overlooked it.

"DR. MAX SYX."

"Tell the gentleman to come in," said the president, and thereupon the attendant threw open the door.

The owner of the mysterious card fixed every eye as he entered. He was several inches more than six feet in height. His complexion was very dark, his eyes were intensely black, bright, and deep-set, his eyebrows were bushy and up-curled at the ends, his sable hair was close-trimmed, and his ears were narrow, pointed at the top, and prominent. He wore black mustaches, covering only half the width of his lip and drawn into projecting needles on each side, while a spiked black beard adorned the middle of his chin.

He smiled as he stepped confidently forward, with a courtly bow, but it was a very disconcerting smile, because it more than half resembled a sneer. This uncommon person did not wait to be addressed.

"I have come to solve your problem," he said, facing President Boon, who had swung round on his pivoted chair.

"The metal!" exclaimed everybody in a breath, and with a unanimity and excitement which would have astonished them if they had been spectators instead of actors of the scene. The tall stranger bowed and smiled again:

"Just so," he said. "What do you think of it?"

"It is beautiful!"

Again the reply came from every mouth simultaneously, and again if the speakers could have been listeners they would have wondered not only at their earnestness, but at their words, for why should they instantly and unanimously pronounce that beautiful which they had not even seen? But every man knew he had seen it, for instinctively their minds reverted to the card and recognized in it the metal referred to. The mesmeric spell seemed once more to fall upon the assemblage, for the financiers noticed nothing remarkable in the next act of the stranger, which was to take a chair, uninvited, at the table, and the moment he sat down he became the presiding officer as naturally as if he had just been elected to that post. They all waited for him to speak, and when he opened his mouth they listened with breathless attention.

His words were of the best English, but there was some peculiarity, which they had already noticed, either in

Garrett P. Serviss

his voice or his manner of enunciation, which struck all of the listeners as denoting a foreigner. But none of them could satisfactorily place him. Neither the Americans, the Englishmen, the Germans, the Frenchmen, the Russians, the Austrians, the Italians, the Spaniards, the Turks, the Japanese, or the Chinese at the board could decide to what race or nationality the stranger belonged.

"This metal," he began, taking the card from Mr. Boon's hand, "I have discovered and named. I call it 'artemisium.' I can produce it, in the pure form, abundantly enough to replace gold, giving it the same relative value that gold possessed when it was the universal standard."

As Dr. Syx spoke he snapped the card with his thumbnail and it fluttered with quivering hues like a humming-bird hovering over a flower. He seemed to await a reply, and President Boon asked:

"What guarantee can you give that the supply would be adequate and continuous?"

"I will conduct a committee of this congress to my mine in the Rocky Mountains, where, in anticipation of the event, I have accumulated enough refined artemisium to provide every civilized land with an amount of coin equivalent to that which it formerly held in gold. I can there satisfy you of my ability to maintain the production."

"But how do we know that this metal of yours will answer the purpose?"

"Try it," was the laconic reply.

"There is another difficulty," pursued the president. "People will not accept a new metal in place of gold unless they are convinced that it possesses equal intrinsic value. They must first become familiar with it, and it must be abundant enough and desirable enough to be used sparingly in the arts, just as gold was."

"I have provided for all that," said the stranger, with one of his disconcerting smiles. "I assure you that there will be no trouble with the people. They will be only too eager to get and to use the metal. Let me show you."

He stepped to the door and immediately returned with two black attendants bearing a large tray filled with articles shaped from the same metal as that of which the card was composed. The financiers all jumped to their feet with exclamations of surprise and admiration, and gathered around the tray, whose dazzling contents lighted up the corner of the room where it had been placed as if the moon were shining there.

There were elegantly formed vases, adorned with artistic figures, embossed and incised, and glowing with delicate colors which shimmered in tiny waves with the slightest motion of the tray. Cups, pins, finger-rings, earrings, watch-chains, combs, studs, lockets, medals, tableware, models of coins - in brief, almost every article in the fabrication of which precious metals have been employed was to be seen there in profusion, and all composed of the strange new metal which everybody on the spot declared was far more splendid than gold.

"Do you think it will answer?" asked Dr. Syx.

"We do," was the unanimous reply.

All then resumed their seats at the table, the tray with its magnificent array having been placed in the centre of the board. This display had a remarkable influence. Confidence awoke in the breasts of the financiers. The dark clouds that had oppressed them rolled off, and the prospect grew decidedly brighter.

"What terms do you demand?" at length asked Mr. Boon, cheerfully rubbing his hands.

"I must have military protection for my mine and reducing works," replied Dr. Syx. "Then I shall ask the return of one per cent, on the circulating medium, together with the privilege of disposing of a certain amount of the metal - to be limited by agreement - to the public for use in the arts. Of the proceeds of this sale I will pay ten per cent. to the government in consideration of its protection."

"But," exclaimed President Boon, "that will make you the richest man who ever lived!"

"Undoubtedly," was the reply.

"Why," added Mr. Boon, opening his eyes wider as the facts continued to dawn upon him, "you will become the financial dictator of the whole earth!"

"Undoubtedly," again responded Dr. Syx, unmoved. "That is what I purpose to become. My discovery entitles me to no less. But, remember, I place myself under government inspection and restriction. I should not be allowed to flood the market, even if I were disposed to do so. But my own interest would restrain me. It is to my advantage that artemisium, once adopted, shall remain stable in value."

A shadow of doubt suddenly crossed the president's face.

"Suppose your secret is discovered," he said. "Surely your mine will not remain the only one. If you, in so short a time, have been able to accumulate an immense quantity of the new metal, it must be extremely abundant. Others will discover it, and then where shall we be?"

While Mr. Boon uttered these words, those who were watching Dr. Syx (as the president was not) resembled persons whose startled eyes are fixed upon a wild beast preparing to spring. As Mr. Boon ceased speaking he turned towards the visitor, and instantly his lips fell apart and his face paled.

Dr. Syx had drawn himself up to his full stature, and his features were distorted with that peculiar mocking smile which had now returned with a concentrated expression of mingled self-confidence and disdain.

"Will you have relief, or not?" he asked in a dry, hard voice. "What can you do? I alone possess the secret which can restore industry and commerce. If you reject my offer, do you think a second one will come?"

President Boon found voice to reply, stammeringly:

"I did not mean to suggest a rejection of the offer. I only wished to inquire if you thought it probable that there would be no repetition of what occurred after gold was found at the south pole?"

"The earth may be full of my metal," returned Dr. Syx, almost fiercely, "but so long as I alone possess the knowledge how to extract it, is it of any more worth than common dirt? But come," he added, after a pause and softening his manner, "I have other schemes. Will you, as representatives of the leading nations, undertake the introduction of artemisium as a substitute for gold, or will you not?"

"Can we not have time for deliberation?" asked President Boon.

"Yes, one hour. Within that time I shall return to learn your decision," replied Dr. Syx, rising and preparing to depart. "I leave these things," pointing to the tray, "in your keeping, and," significantly, "I trust your decision will be a wise one."

His curious smile again curved his lips and shot the ends of his mustache upward, and the influence of that smile remained in the room when he had closed the door behind him. The financiers gazed at one another for several minutes in silence, then they turned towards the coruscating metal that filled the tray.

III

THE GRAND TETON MINE

Away on the western border of Wyoming, in the all but inaccessible heart of the Rocky Mountains, three mighty brothers, "The Big Tetons," look perpendicularly into the blue eye of Jenny's Lake, lying at the bottom of the profound depression among the mountains called Jackson's Hole. Bracing against one another for support, these remarkable peaks lift their granite spires from 12,000 to nearly 14,000 feet into the blue dome that arches the crest of the continent. Their sides, and especially those of their chief, the Grand Teton, are streaked with glaciers, which shine like silver trappings when the morning sun comes up above the wilderness of mountains stretching away eastward from the hole.

When the first white men penetrated this wonderful region, and one of them bestowed his wife's name upon Jenny's Lake, they were intimidated by the Grand Teton. It made their flesh creep, accustomed though they were to rough scrambling among mountain gorges and on the brows of immense precipices, when they glanced up the face of the peak, where the cliffs fall, one below another, in a series of breathless descents, and imagined themselves clinging for dear life to those skyey battlements.

But when, in 1872, Messrs. Stevenson and Langford finally reached the top of the Grand Teton - the only successful members of a party of nine practised climbers who had started together from the bottom – they found there a little rectangular enclosure, made by piling up rocks, six or seven feet across and three feet in height, bearing evidences of great age, and indicating that the red Indians had, for some unknown purpose, resorted to the summit of this tremendous peak long before the white men invaded their mountains. Yet neither the Indians nor the whites ever really conquered the Teton, for above the highest point that they attained rises a granite buttress, whose smooth vertical sides seemed to them to defy everything but wings.

Winding across the sage-covered floor of Jackson's Hole runs the Shoshone, or Snake River, which takes its rise from Jackson's Lake at the northern end of the basin, and then, as if shrinking from the threatening brows of the Tetons, whose fall would block its progress, makes a detour of one hundred miles around the buttressed heights of the range before it finds a clear way across Idaho, and so on to the Columbia River and the Pacific Ocean.

On a July morning, about a month after the visit of Dr. Max Syx to the assembled financiers in New York, a party of twenty horsemen, following a mountain-trail, arrived on the eastern margin of Jackson's Hole, and pausing upon a commanding eminence, with exclamations of wonder, glanced across the great depression, where lay the shining coils of the Snake River, at the towering forms of the Tetons, whose ice-striped cliffs flashed lightnings in the sunshine. Even the impassive broncos that the party rode lifted their heads inquiringly, and snorted as if in equine astonishment at the magnificent spectacle.

One familiar with the place would have noticed something, which, to his mind, would have seemed more surprising than the pageantry of the mountains in their morning sun-bath. Curling above one of the wild gorges that cut the lower slopes of the Tetons was a thick black smoke, which, when lifted by a passing breeze, obscured the precipices half-way to the summit of the peak.

Had the Grand Teton become a volcano? Certainly no hunting or exploring party could make a smoke like that. But a word from the leader of the party of horsemen explained the mystery.

"There is my mill, and the mine is underneath it."

The speaker was Dr. Syx, and his companions were members of the financial congress. When he quitted their presence in New York, with the promise to return within an hour for their reply, he had no doubt in his own mind what that reply would be. He knew they would accept his proposition, and they did. No time was then lost in communicating with the various governments, and arrangements were quickly perfected whereby, in case the inspection of Dr. Syx's mine and its resources proved satisfactory, America and Europe should unite in adopting the new metal as the basis of their coinage. As soon as this stage in the negotiations was reached, it only remained to send a committee of financiers and metallurgists, in company with Dr. Syx, to the Rocky Mountains. They started under the doctor's guidance, completing the last stage of their journey on horseback.

"An inspection of the records at Washington," Dr. Syx continued, addressing the horsemen, "will show that I have filed a claim covering ten acres of ground around the mouth of my mine. This was done as soon as I had discovered the metal. The filing of the claim and the subsequent proceedings which perfected my ownership attracted no attention, because everybody was thinking of the south pole and its gold-fields."

The party gathered closer around Dr. Syx and listened to his words with silent attention, while their horses rubbed noses and jingled their gold-mounted trappings.

"As soon as I had legally protected myself," he continued, "I employed a force of men, transported my machinery and material across the mountains, erected my furnaces, and opened the mine. I was safe from intrusion, and even from idle curiosity, for the reason I have just mentioned. In fact, so exclusive was the attraction of the new gold-fields that I had difficulty in obtaining workmen, and finally I sent to Africa and engaged negroes, whom I placed in charge of trustworthy foremen. Accordingly, with half a dozen exceptions, you will see only black men at the mine."

"And with their aid you have mined enough metal to supply the mints of the world?" asked President Boon.

"Exactly so," was the reply. "But I no longer employ the large force which I needed at first."

"How much metal have you on hand? I am aware that you have already answered this question during our preliminary negotiations, but I ask it again for the benefit of some members of our party who were not present then."

"I shall show you to-day," said Dr. Syx, with his curious smile, "2500 tons of refined artemisium, stacked in rock-cut vaults under the Grand Teton."

"And you have dared to collect such inconceivable wealth in one place?"

"You forget that it is not wealth until the people have learned to value it, and the governments have put their stamp upon it."

"True, but how did you arrive at the proper moment?"

"Easily. I first ascertained that before the Antarctic discoveries the world contained altogether about 16,000 tons of gold, valued at $450,000 per ton, or $7,200,000,000 worth all told. Now my metal weighs, bulk for bulk, one-quarter as much as gold. It might be reckoned at the same intrinsic value per ton, but I have considered it preferable to take advantage of the smaller weight of the new metal, which permits us to make coins of the same size as the old ones, but only one-quarter as heavy, by giving to artemisium four times the value per ton that gold had. Thus only 4000 tons of the new metal are required to supply the place of the 16,000 tons of gold. The 2500 tons which I already have on hand are more than enough for coinage. The rest I can supply as fast as needed."

The party did not wait for further explanations. They were eager to see the wonderful mine and the store of treasure. Spurs were applied, and they galloped down the steep trail, forded the Snake River, and, skirting the shore of Jenny's Lake, soon found themselves gazing up the headlong slopes and dizzy parapets of the Grand Teton. Dr. Syx led them by a steep ascent to the mouth of the canyon, above one of whose walls stood his mill, and where the "Champ! Champ!" of a powerful engine saluted their ears.

IV

THE WEALTH OF THE WORLD

An electric light shot its penetrating rays into a gallery cut through virgin rock and running straight towards the heart of the Teton. The centre of the gallery was occupied by a narrow railway, on which a few flat cars, propelled by electric power, passed to and fro. Black-skinned and silent workmen rode on the cars, both when they came laden with broken masses of rock from the farther end of the tunnel and when they returned empty.

Suddenly, to an eye situated a little way within the gallery, appeared at the entrance the dark face of Dr. Syx, wearing its most discomposing smile, and a moment later the broader countenance of President Boon loomed in the electric glare beside the doctor's black framework of eyebrows and mustache. Behind them were grouped the other visiting financiers.

"This tunnel," said Dr. Syx, "leads to the mine head, where the ore-bearing rock is blasted."

As he spoke a hollow roar issued from the depths of the mountain, followed in a short time by a gust of foul air.

"You probably will not care to go in there," said the doctor, "and, in fact, it is very uncomfortable. But we shall follow the next car-load to the smelter, and you can witness the reduction of the ore."

Accordingly when another car came rumbling out of the tunnel, with its load of cracked rock, they all accompanied it into an adjoining apartment, where it was cast into a metallic shute, through which, they were informed, it reached the furnace.

"While it is melting," explained Dr. Syx, "certain elements, the nature of which I must beg to keep secret, are mixed with the ore, causing chemical action which results in the extraction of the metal. Now let me show you pure artemisium issuing from the furnace."

He led the visitors through two apartments into a third, one side of which was walled by the front of a furnace. From this projected two or three small spouts, and iridescent streams of molten metal fell from the spouts into earthen receptacles from which the blazing liquid was led, like flowing iron, into a system of molds, where it was allowed to cool and harden.

The financiers looked on wondering, and their astonishment grew when they were conducted into the rock-cut store-rooms beneath, where they saw metallic ingots glowing like gigantic opals in the light which Dr. Syx turned on. They were piled in rows along the walls as high as a man could reach. A very brief inspection sufficed to convince the visitors that Dr. Syx was able to perform all that he promised. Although they had not penetrated the secret of his process of reducing the ore, yet they had seen the metal flowing from the furnace, and the piles of ingots proved conclusively that he had uttered no vain boast when he said he could give the world a new coinage.

But President Boon, being himself a metallurgist, desired to inspect the mysterious ore a little more closely. Possibly he was thinking that if another mine was destined to be discovered he might as well be the discoverer as anybody. Dr. Syx attempted no concealment, but his smile became more than usually scornful as he stopped a laden car and invited the visitors to help themselves.

"I think," he said, "that I have struck the only lode of this ore in the Teton, or possibly in this part of the world, but I don't know for certain. There may be plenty of it only waiting to be found. That, however, doesn't trouble me. The great point is that nobody except myself knows how to extract the metal."

Mr. Boon closely examined the chunk of rock which he had taken from the car. Then he pulled a lens from his pocket, with a deprecatory glance at Dr. Syx.

"Oh, that's all right," said the latter, with a laugh, the first that these gentlemen had ever heard from his lips, and it almost made them shudder; "put it to every test, examine it with the microscope, with fire, with electricity, with the spectroscope - in every way you can think of! I assure you it is worth your while!"

Again Dr. Syx uttered his freezing laugh, passing into the familiar smile, which had now become an undisguised mock.

"Upon my word," said Mr. Boon, taking his eye from

the lens, "I see no sign of any metal here!"

"Look at the green specks!" cried the doctor, snatching the specimen from the president's hand. "That's it! That's artemisium! But it's of no use unless you can get it out and purify it, which is my secret!"

For the third time Dr. Syx laughed, and his merriment affected the visitors so disagreeably that they showed impatience to be gone. Immediately he changed his manner.

"Come into my office," he said, with a return to the graciousness which had characterized him ever since the party started from New York.

When they were all seated, and the doctor had handed round a box of cigars, he resumed the conversation in his most amiable manner.

"You see, gentlemen," he said, turning a piece of ore in his fingers, "artemisium is like aluminum. It can only be obtained in the metallic form by a special process. While these greenish particles, which you may perhaps mistake for chrysolite, or some similar unisilicate, really contain the precious metal, they are not entirely composed of it. The process by which I separate out the metallic element while the ore is passing through the furnace is, in truth, quite simple, and its very simplicity guards my secret. Make your minds easy as to over-production. A man is as likely to jump over the moon as to find me out."

"But," he continued, again changing his manner, "we have had business enough for one day; now for a little recreation." While speaking the doctor pressed a button on his desk, and the room, which was illuminated by electric lamps - for there were no windows in the building - suddenly became dark, except part of one wall, where a broad area of light appeared. Dr. Syx's voice had become very soothing when next he spoke: "I am fond of amusing myself with a peculiar form of the magic-lantern, which I invented some years ago, and which I have never exhibited except for the entertainment of my friends. The pictures will appear upon the wall, the apparatus being concealed."

He had hardly ceased speaking when the illuminated space seemed to melt away, leaving a great opening, through which the spectators looked as if into another world on the opposite side of the wall. For a minute or two they could not clearly discern what was presented; then, gradually, the flitting scenes and figures became more distinct until the lifelikeness of the spectacle absorbed their whole attention.

Before them passed, in panoramic review, a sunny land, filled with brilliant-hued vegetation, and dotted with villages and cities which were bright with light-colored buildings. People appeared moving through the scenes, as in a cinematograph exhibition, but with infinitely more semblance of reality. In fact, the pictures, blending one into another, seemed to be life itself. Yet it was not an earth-like scene. The colors of the passing landscape were such as no man in the room had ever beheld; and the people, tall, round-limbed, with florid complexion, golden hair, and brilliant eyes and lips, were indescribably beautiful and graceful in all their movements.

From the land the view passed out to sea, and bright blue waves, edged with creaming foam, ran swiftly under the spectator's eyes, and occasionally, driven before light winds, appeared fleets of daintily shaped vessels, which reminded the beholder, by their flashing wings, of the feigned "ship of pearl."

After the fairy ships and breezy sea views came a long, curving line of coast, brilliant with coral sands, and indented by frequent bays, along whose enchanting shores lay pleasant towns, the landscapes behind them splendid with groves, meadows, and streams.

Presently the shifting photographic tape, or whatever the mechanism may have been, appeared to have settled upon a chosen scene, and there it rested. A broad champaign reached away to distant sapphire mountains, while the foreground was occupied by a magnificent house, resembling a large country villa, fronted with a garden, shaded by bowers and festoons of huge, brilliant flowers. Birds of radiant plumage flitted among the trees and blossoms, and then appeared a company of gayly attired people, including many young girls, who joined hands and danced in a ring, apparently with shouts of laughter, while a group of musicians standing near thrummed and blew upon curiously shaped instruments.

Suddenly the shadow of a dense cloud flitted across the scene; whereupon the brilliant birds flew away with screams of terror which almost seemed to reach the ears of the onlookers through the wall. An expression of horror came over the faces of the people. The children broke from their merry circle and ran for protection to their elders. The utmost confusing and whelming terror were evidenced for a moment - then the ground split asunder, and the house and the garden, with all their living occupants were swallowed by an awful chasm which opened just where they had stood. The great rent ran in a widening line across the sunlit landscape until it reached the horizon, when the distant mountains crumbled, clouds poured in from all sides at once, and billows of flame burst through them as they veiled the scene.

But in another instant the commotion was over, and the world whose curious spectacles had been enacted as if on the other side of a window, seemed to retreat swiftly into space, until at last, emerging from a fleecy cloud, it reappeared in the form of the full moon hanging in the sky, but larger than is its wont, with its dry ocean-beds, its keen-spired peaks, its ragged mountain ranges, its gaping chasms, its immense crater rings, and Tycho, the chief of them all, shooting raylike streaks across the scarred face of the abandoned lunar globe. The show was ended, and Dr. Syx, turning on only a partial illumination in the room, rose slowly to his feet, his tall form appearing strangely magnified in the gloom, and invited his bewildered guests to accompany him to his house, outside the mill, where he said dinner awaited them. As they emerged into daylight they acted like persons just aroused from an opiate dream.

V

WONDERS OF THE NEW METAL

Within a twelvemonth after the visit of President Boon and his fellow financiers to the mine in the Grand Teton a railway had been constructed from Jackson's Hole, connecting with one of the Pacific lines, and the distribution of the new metal was begun. All of Dr. Syx's terms had been accepted. United States troops occupied a permanent encampment on the upper waters of the Snake River, to afford protection, and as the consignments of precious ingots were hurried east and west on guarded trains, the mints all over the world resumed their activity. Once more a common monetary standard prevailed, and commerce revived as if touched by a magic wand.

Artemisium quickly won its way in popular favor. Its matchless beauty alone was enough. Not only was it gladly accepted in the form of money, but its success was instantaneous in the arts. Dr. Syx and the inspectors representing the various nations found it difficult to limit the output to the agreed upon amount. The demand was incessant.

Goldsmiths and jewellers continually discovered new excellences in the wonderful metal. Its properties of translucence and refraction enabled skilful artists to perform marvels. By suitable management a chain of artemisium could be made to resemble a string of vari-colored gems, each separate link having a tint of its own, while, as the wearer moved, delicate complementary colors chased one another, in rapid undulation, from end to end.

A fresh charm was added by the new metal to the personal adornment of women, and an enhanced splendor to the pageants of society. Gold in its palmiest days had never enjoyed such a vogue. A crowded reception room or a dinner party where artemisium abounded possessed an indescribable atmosphere of luxury and richness, refined in quality, yet captivating to every sense. Imaginative persons went so far as to aver that the sight and presence of the metal exercised a strangely soothing and dreamy power over the mind, like the influence of moonlight streaming through the tree-tops on a still, balmy night.

The public curiosity in regard to the origin of artemisium was boundless. The various nations published official bulletins in which the general facts - omitting, of course, such incidents as the singular exhibition seen by the visiting financiers on the wall of Dr. Syx's office - were detailed to gratify the universal desire for information.

President Boon not only submitted the specimens of ore-bearing rock which he had brought from the mine to careful analysis, but also appealed to several of the greatest living chemists and mineralogists to aid him; but they were all equally mystified. The green substance contained in the ore, although differing slightly from ordinary chrysolite, answered all the known tests of that mineral. It was remembered, however, that Dr. Syx had said that they would be likely to mistake the substance for chrysolite, and the result of their experiments justified his prediction. Evidently the doctor had gone a stone's-cast beyond the chemistry of the day, and, just as evidently, he did not mean to reveal his discovery for the benefit of science, nor for the benefit of any pockets except his own.

Notwithstanding the failure of the chemists to extract anything from Dr. Syx's ore, the public at large never doubted that the secret would be discovered in good time, and thousands of prospectors flocked to the Teton Mountains in search of the ore. And without much difficulty they found it. Evidently the doctor had been mistaken in thinking that his mine might be the only one. The new miners hurried specimens of the green-speckled rock to the chemical laboratories for experimentation, and meanwhile began to lay up stores of the ore in anticipation of the time when the proper way to extract the metal should be discovered.

But, alas! that time did not come. The fresh ore proved to be as refractory as that which had been obtained from Dr. Syx. But in the midst of the universal disappointment there came a new sensation.

One morning the newspapers glared with a despatch from Grand Teton station announcing that the metal itself had been discovered by prospectors on the eastern slope of the main peak.

"It outcrops in many places," ran the despatch, "and many small nuggets have been picked out of crevices in the rocks."

The excitement produced by this news was even greater than when gold was discovered at the south pole. Again a mad rush was made for the Tetons. The heights around Jackson's Hole and the shores of Jackson's and Jenny's lakes were quickly dotted with camps, and the military force had to be doubled to keep off the curious, and occasionally menacing, crowds which gathered in the vicinity and seemed bent on unearthing the great secret locked behind the windowless walls of the mill, where the column of black smoke and the roar of the engine served as reminders of the incredible wealth which the sole possessor of that secret was rolling up.

This time no mistake had been made. It was a fact that the metal, in virgin purity, had been discovered scattered in various places on the ledges of the Grand Teton. In a little while thousands had obtained specimens with their own hands. The quantity was distressingly small, considering the number and the eagerness of the seekers, but that it was genuine artemisium not even Dr. Syx could have denied. He, however, made no attempt to deny it.

"Yes," he said, when questioned, "I find that I have been deceived. At first I thought the metal existed only in the form of the green ore, but of late I have come upon veins of pure artemisium in my mine. I am glad for your sakes, but sorry for my own. Still, it may turn out that there is no great amount of free artemisium after all."

While the doctor talked in this manner close observers detected a lurking sneer which his acquaintances had not noticed since artemisium was first adopted as the money basis of the world.

The crowd that swarmed upon the mountain quickly exhausted all of the visible supply of the metal. Sometimes they found it in a thin stratum at the bottom of crevices, where it could be detached in opalescent plates and leaves of the thickness of paper. These superficial deposits evidently might have been formed from water holding the metal in solution. Occasionally, deep cracks contained nuggets and wiry masses which looked as if they had run together when molten.

The most promising spots were soon staked out in miners' claims, machinery was procured, stock companies were formed, and borings were begun. The enthusiasm arising from the earlier finds and the flattering surface indications caused everybody to work with feverish haste and energy, and within two months one hundred tunnels were piercing the mountain.

For a long time nobody was willing to admit the truth which gradually forced itself upon the attention of the miners. The deeper they went the scarcer became the indications of artemisium! In fact, such deposits as were found were confined to fissures near the surface. But Dr. Syx continued to report a surprising increase in the amount of free metal in his mine, and this encouraged all who had not exhausted their capital to push on their tunnels in the hope of finally striking a vein. At length, however, the smaller operators gave up in despair, until only one heavily capitalized company remained at work.

VI

A STRANGE DISCOVERY

"It is my belief that Dr. Max Syx is a deceiver."

The person who uttered this opinion was a young engineer, Andrew Hall, who had charge of the operations of one of the mining companies which were driving tunnels into the Grand Teton.

"What do you mean by that?" asked President Boon, who was the principal backer of the enterprise.

"I mean," replied Hall, "that there is no free metal in this mountain, and Dr. Syx knows there is none."

"But he is getting it himself from his mine," retorted President Boon.

"So he says, but who has seen it? No one is admitted into the Syx mine, his foremen are forbidden to talk, and his workmen are specially imported negroes who do not understand the English language."

"But," persisted Mr. Boon, "how, then, do you account for the nuggets scattered over the mountain? And, beside, what object could Dr. Syx have in pretending that there is free metal to be had for the digging?"

Garrett P. Serviss

"He may have salted the mountain, for all I know," said Hall. "As for his object, I confess I am entirely in the dark; but, for all that, I am convinced that we shall find no more metal if we dig ten miles for it."

"Nonsense," said the president; "if we keep on we shall strike it. Did not Dr. Syx himself admit that he found no free artemisium until his tunnel had reached the core of the peak? We must go as deep as he has gone before we give up."

"I fear the depths he attains are beyond most people's reach," was Hall's answer, while a thoughtful look crossed his clear-cut brow, "but since you desire it, of course the work shall go on. I should like, however, to change the direction of the tunnel."

"Certainly," replied Mr. Boon; "bore in whatever direction you think proper, only don't despair."

About a month after this conversation Andrew Hall, with whom a community of tastes in many things had made me intimately acquainted, asked me one morning to accompany him into his tunnel.

"I want to have a trusty friend at my elbow," he said, "for, unless I am a dreamer, something remarkable will happen within the next hour, and two witnesses are better than one."

I knew Hall was not the person to make such a remark carelessly, and my curiosity was intensely excited, but, knowing his peculiarities, I did not press him for an explanation. When we arrived at the head of the tunnel I was surprised at finding no workmen there.

"I stopped blasting some time ago," said Hall, in explanation, "for a reason which, I hope, will become evident to you very soon. Lately I have been boring very slowly, and yesterday I paid off the men and dismissed them with the announcement, which, I am confident, President Boon will sanction after he hears my report of this morning's work, that the tunnel is abandoned. You see, I am now using a drill which I can manage without assistance. I believe the work is almost completed, and I want you to witness the end of it."

He then carefully applied the drill, which noiselessly screwed its nose into the rock. When it had sunk to a depth of a few inches he withdrew it, and, taking a hand-drill capable of making a hole not more than an eighth of an inch in diameter, cautiously began boring in the centre of the larger cavity. He had made hardly a hundred turns of the handle when the drill shot through the rock! A gratified smile illuminated his features, and he said in a suppressed voice:

"Don't be alarmed; I'm going to put out the light."

Instantly we were in complete darkness, but being close at Hall's side I could detect his movements. He pulled out the drill, and for half a minute remained motionless as if listening. There was no sound.

"I must enlarge the opening," he whispered, and immediately the faint grating of a sharp tool cutting through the rock informed me of his progress.

"There," at last he said, "I think that will do; now for a look."

I could tell that he had placed his eye at the hole and was gazing with breathless attention. Presently he pulled my sleeve.

"Put your eye here," he whispered, pushing me into the proper position for looking through the hole.

At first I could discern nothing except a smoky blue glow. But soon my vision cleared a little, and then I perceived that I was gazing into a narrow tunnel which met ours directly end to end. Glancing along the axis of this gallery I saw, some two hundred yards away, a faint light which evidently indicated the mouth of the tunnel.

At the end where we had met it the mysterious tunnel was considerably widened at one side, as if the excavators had started to change direction and then abandoned the work, and in this elbow I could just see the outlines of two or three flat cars loaded with broken stone, while a heap of the same material lay near them. Through the centre of the tunnel ran a railway track.

"Do you know what you are looking at?" asked Hall in my ear.

"I begin to suspect," I replied, "that you have accidentally run into Dr. Syx's mine."

"If Dr. Syx had been on his guard this accident wouldn't have happened," replied Hall, with an almost inaudible chuckle.

"I heard you remark a month ago," I said, "that you were changing the direction of your tunnel. Has this been the aim of your labors ever since?"

"You have hit it," he replied. "Long ago I became convinced that my company was throwing away its money in a vain attempt to strike a lode of pure artemisium. But President Boon has great faith in Dr. Syx, and would not give up the work. So I adopted what I regarded as the only practicable method of proving the truth of my opinion and saving the company's funds. An electric indicator, of my invention, enabled me to locate the Syx tunnel when I got near it, and I have met it end on, and opened this peep-hole in order to observe the doctor's operations. I feel that such spying is entirely justified in the circumstances. Although I cannot yet explain just how or why I feel sure that Dr. Syx was the cause of the sudden discovery of the surface nuggets, and that he has encouraged the miners for his own ends, until he has brought ruin to thousands who have spent their last cent in driving useless tunnels into this mountain. It is a righteous thing to expose him."

"But," I interposed, "I do not see that you have exposed anything yet except the interior of a tunnel."

"You will see more clearly after a while," was the reply.

Hall now placed his eye again at the aperture, and was unable entirely to repress the exclamation that rose to his lips. He remained staring through the hole for several minutes without uttering a word. Presently I noticed that the lenses of his eye were illuminated by a ray of light coming through the hole, but he did not stir.

After a long inspection he suddenly applied his ear to the hole and listened intently for at least five minutes. Not a sound was audible to me, but, by an occasional pressure of the hand, Hall signified that some important disclosure was reaching his sense of hearing. At length he removed his ear.

"Pardon me," he whispered, "for keeping you so long in waiting, but what I have just seen and overheard was of a nature to admit of no interruption. He is still talking, and by pressing your ear against the hole you may be able to catch what he says."

"Who is 'he'?"

"Look for yourself."

I placed my eye at the aperture, and almost recoiled with the violence of my surprise. The tunnel before me was brilliantly illuminated, and within three feet of the wall of rock behind which we crouched stood Dr. Syx, his dark profile looking almost satanic in the sharp contrast of light and shadow. He was talking to one of his foremen, and the two were the only visible occupants of the tunnel. Putting my ear to the little opening, I heard his words distinctly:

 - "end of their rope. Well, they've spent a pretty lot of money for their experience, and I rather think we shall not be troubled again by artemisium-seekers for some time to come."

The doctor's voice ceased, and instantly I clapped my eye to the hole. He had changed his position so that his black eyes now looked straight at the aperture. My heart was in my mouth, for at first I believed from his expression that he had detected the gleam of my eyeball. But if so, he probably mistook it for a bit of mica in the rock, and paid no further attention. Then his lips moved, and I put my ear again to the hole. He seemed to be replying to a question that the foreman had asked.

"If they do," he said, "they will never guess the real secret."

Thereupon he turned on his heel, kicked a bit of rock off the track, and strode away towards the entrance. The foreman paused long enough to turn out the electric lamp, and then followed the doctor.

"Well," asked Hall, "what have you heard?"

I told him everything.

"It fully corroborates the evidence of my own eyes and ears," he remarked, "and we may count ourselves extremely lucky. It is not likely that Dr. Syx will be heard a second time proclaiming his deception with his own lips. It is plain that he was led to talk as he did to the foreman on account of the latter's having informed him of the sudden discharge of my men this morning. Their presence within ear-shot of our hiding-place during their conversation was, of course, pure accident, and so you can see how kind fortune has been to us. I expected to have to watch and listen and form deductions for a week, at least, before getting the information which five lucky minutes have placed in our hands."

While he was speaking my companion busied himself in carefully plugging up the hole in the rock. When it was closed to his satisfaction he turned on the light in our tunnel.

"Did you observe," he asked, "that there was a second tunnel?"

"What do you say?"

"When the light was on in there I saw the mouth of a smaller tunnel entering the main one behind the cars on the right. Did you notice it?"

"Oh yes," I replied. "I did observe some kind of a dark hole there, but I paid no attention to it because I was so absorbed in the doctor."

"Well," rejoined Hall, smiling, "it was worth considerably more than a glance. As a subject of thought I find it even more absorbing than Dr. Syx. Did you see the track in it?"

"No," I had to acknowledge, "I did not notice that. But," I continued, a little piqued by his manner, "being a branch of the main tunnel, I don't see anything remarkable in its having a track also."

"It was rather dim in that hole," said Hall, still smiling in a somewhat provoking way, "but the railroad track was there plain enough. And, whether you think it remarkable or not, I should like to lay you a wager that that track leads to a secret worth a dozen of the one we have just overheard."

"My good friend," I retorted, still smarting a little, "I shall not presume to match my stupidity against your perspicacity. I haven't cat's eyes in the dark."

Hall immediately broke out laughing, and, slapping me good-naturedly on the shoulder, exclaimed:

"Come, come now! If you go to kicking back at a fellow like that, I shall be sorry I ever undertook this adventure."

VII

A MYSTERY INDEED!

When President Boon had heard our story he promptly approved Hall's dismissal of the men. He expressed great surprise that Dr. Syx should have resorted to a deception which had been so disastrous to innocent people, and at first he talked of legal proceedings. But, after thinking the matter over, he concluded that Syx was too powerful to be attacked with success, especially when the only evidence against him was that he had claimed to find artemisium in his mine at a time when, as everybody knew, artemisium actually was found outside the mine. There was no apparent motive for the deception, and no proof of malicious intent. In short, Mr. Boon decided that the best thing for him and his stockholders to do was to keep silent about their losses and await events. And, at Hall's suggestion, he also determined to say nothing to anybody about the discovery we had made.

"It could do no good," said Hall, in making the suggestion, "and it might spoil a plan I have in mind."

"What plan?" asked the president.

"I prefer not to tell just yet," was the reply.

I observed that, in our interview with Mr. Boon, Hall made no reference to the side tunnel to which he had appeared to attach so much importance, and I concluded that he now regarded it as lacking significance. In this I was mistaken.

A few days afterwards I received an invitation from Hall to accompany him once more into the abandoned tunnel.

"I have found out what that sidetrack means," he said, "and it has plunged me into another mystery so dark and profound that I cannot see my way through it. I must beg you to say no word to any one concerning the things I am about to show you."

I gave the required promise, and we entered the tunnel, which nobody had visited since our former adventure. Having extinguished our lamp, my companion opened the peep-hole, and a thin ray of light streamed through from the tunnel on the opposite side of the wall. He applied his eye to the hole.

"Yes," he said, quickly stepping back and pushing me into his place, "they are still at it. Look, and tell me what you see."

"I see," I replied, after placing my eye at the aperture, "a gang of men unloading a car which has just come out of the side tunnel, and putting its contents upon another car standing on the track of the main tunnel."

"Yes, and what are they handling?"

"Why, ore, of course."

"And do you see nothing significant in that?"

"To be sure!" I exclaimed. "Why, that ore - "

"Hush! hush!" admonished Hall, putting his hand over my mouth; "don't talk so loud. Now go on, in a whisper."

"The ore," I resumed, "may have come back from the furnace-room, because the side tunnel turns off so as to run parallel with the other."

"It not only may have come back, it actually has come back," said Hall.

"How can you be sure?"

"Because I have been over the track, and know that it leads to a secret apartment directly under the furnace in which Dr. Syx pretends to melt the ore!"

For a minute after hearing this avowal I was speechless.

"Are you serious?" I asked at length.

"Perfectly serious. Run your finger along the rock here. Do you perceive a seam? Two days ago, after seeing what you have just witnessed in the Syx tunnel, I carefully cut out a section of the wall, making an aperture large enough to crawl through, and, when I knew the workmen were asleep, I crept in there and examined both tunnels from end to end. But in solving one mystery I have run myself into another infinitely more perplexing."

"How is that?"

"Why does Dr. Syx take such elaborate pains to deceive his visitors, and also the government officers? It is now plain that he conducts no mining operations whatever. This mine of his is a gigantic blind. Whenever inspectors or scientific curiosity seekers visit his mill his mute workmen assume the air of being very busy, the cars laden with his so-called 'ore' rumble out of the tunnel, and their contents are ostentatiously poured into the furnace, or appear to be poured into it, really dropping into a receptacle beneath, to be carried back into the mine again. And then the doctor leads his gulled visitors around to the other side of the furnace and shows them the molten metal coming out in streams. Now what does it all mean? That's what I'd like to find out. What's his game? For, mark you, if he doesn't get artemisium from this pretended ore, he gets it from some other source, and right on this spot, too. There is no doubt about that. The whole world is supplied by Syx's furnace, and Syx feeds his furnace with something that comes from his ten acres of Grand Teton rock. What is that something? How does he get it, and where does he hide it? These are the things I should like to find out."

"Well," I replied, "I fear I can't help you."

"But the difference between you and me," he retorted, "is that you can go to sleep over it, while I shall never get another good night's rest so long as this black mystery remains unsolved."

"What will you do?"

"I don't know exactly what. But I've got a dim idea

which may take shape after a while."

Hall was silent for some time; then he suddenly asked:

"Did you ever hear of that queer magic-lantern show with which Dr. Syx entertained Mr. Boon and the members of the financial commission in the early days of the artemisium business?"

"Yes, I've heard the story, but I don't think it was ever made public. The newspapers never got hold of it."

"No, I believe not. Odd thing, wasn't it?"

"Why, yes, very odd, but just like the doctor's eccentric ways, though. He's always doing something to astonish somebody, without any apparent earthly reason. But what put you in mind of that?"

"Free artemisium put me in mind of it," replied Hall, quizzically.

"I don't see the connection."

"I'm not sure that I do either, but when you are dealing with Dr. Syx nothing is too improbable to be thought of."

Hall thereupon fell to musing again, while we returned to the entrance of the tunnel. After he had made everything secure, and slipped the key into his pocket, my companion remarked:

"Don't you think it would be best to keep this latest discovery to ourselves?"

"Certainly."

"Because," he continued, "nobody would be benefited just now by knowing what we know, and to expose the worthlessness of the 'ore' might cause a panic. The public is a queer animal, and never gets scared at just the thing you expect will alarm it, but always at something else."

We had shaken hands and were separating when Hall stopped me.

"Do you believe in alchemy?" he asked.

"That's an odd question from you," I replied. "I thought alchemy was exploded long ago."

"Well," he said, slowly, "I suppose it has been exploded, but then, you know, an explosion may sometimes be a kind of instantaneous education, breaking up old things but revealing new ones."

Garrett P. Serviss

VIII

MORE OF DR. SYX'S MAGIC

Important business called me East soon after the meeting with Hall described in the foregoing chapter, and before I again saw the Grand Teton very stirring events had taken place.

As the reader is aware, Dr. Syx's agreement with the various governments limited the output of his mine. An international commission, continually in session in New York, adjusted the differences arising among the nations concerning financial affairs, and allotted to each the proper amount of artemisium for coinage. Of course, this amount varied from time to time, but a fair average could easily be maintained. The gradual increase of wealth, in houses, machinery, manufac-tured and artistic products called for a corresponding increase in the circulating medium; but this, too, was easily provided for. An equally painstaking supervision was exercised over the amount of the precious metal which Dr. Syx was permitted to supply to the markets for use in the arts. On this side, also, the demand gradually increased; but the wonderful Teton mine seemed equal to all calls upon its resources.

After the failure of the mining operations there was a moderate revival of the efforts to reduce the Teton ore, but no success cheered the experimenters. Prospectors also wandered all over the earth looking for pure artemisium, but in vain. The general public, knowing nothing of what Hall had discovered, and still believing Syx's story that he also had found pure artemisium in his mine, accounted for the failure of the tunnelling operations on the supposition that the metal, in a free state, was excessively rare, and that Dr. Syx had had the luck to strike the only vein of it that the Grand Teton contained. As if to give countenance to this opinion, Dr. Syx now announced, in the most public manner, that he had been deceived again, and that the vein of free metal he had struck being exhausted, no other had appeared. Accordingly, he said, he must henceforth rely exclusively, as in the beginning, upon reduction of the ore.

Artemisium had proved itself an immense boon to mankind, and the new era of commercial prosperity which it had ushered in already exceeded everything that the world had known in the past. School-children learned that human civilization had taken five great strides, known respectively, beginning at the bottom, as the "age of stone," the "age of bronze," the "age of iron," the "age of gold," and the "age of artemisium."

Nevertheless, sources of dissatisfaction finally began to appear, and, after the nature of such things, they developed with marvellous rapidity. People began to grumble about "contraction of the currency." In every country there arose a party which demanded "free money." Demagogues pointed to the brief reign of paper money after the demonetization of gold as a happy period, when the people had enjoyed their rights, and the "money barons" - borrowing a term from nineteenth-century history - were kept at bay.

Then came denunciations of the international commission for restricting the coinage. Dr. Syx was described as "a devil-fish sucking the veins of the planet and holding it helpless in the grasp of his tentacular billions." In the United States meetings of agitators passed furious resolutions, denouncing the government, assailing the rich, cursing Dr. Syx, and calling upon "the oppressed" to rise and "take their own." The final outcome was, of course, violence. Mobs had to be suppressed by military force. But the most dramatic scene in the tragedy occurred at the Grand Teton. Excited by inflammatory speeches and printed documents, several thousand armed men assembled in the neighborhood of Jenny's Lake and prepared to attack the Syx mine. For some reason the military guard had been depleted, and the mob, under the leadership of a man named Bings, who showed no little talent as a commander and strategist, surprised the small force of soldiers and locked them up in their own guard-house.

Telegraphic communication having been cut off by the astute Bings, a fierce attack was made on the mine. The assailants swarmed up the sides of the canyon, and attempted to break in through the foundation of the buildings. But the masonry was stronger than they had anticipated, and the attack failed. Sharp-shooters then climbed the neighboring heights, and kept up an incessant peppering of the walls with conical bullets driven at four thousand feet per second.

No reply came from the gloomy structure. The huge column of black smoke rose uninterruptedly into the sky, and the noise of the great engine never ceased for an instant. The mob gathered closer on all sides and redoubled the fire of the rifles, to which was now added the belching of several machine-guns. Ragged holes began to appear in the walls, and at the sight of these the assailants yelled with delight. It was evident that, the mill could not long withstand so destructive a bombardment. If the besiegers had possessed artillery they would have knocked the buildings into splinters within twenty minutes. As it was, they would need a whole day to win their victory.

Suddenly it became evident that the besieged were about to take a hand in the fight. Thus far they had not shown themselves or fired a shot, but now a movement was perceived on the roof, and the projecting arms of some kind of machinery became visible. Many marksmen concentrated their fire upon the mysterious objects, but apparently with little effect. Bings, mounted on a rock, so as to command a clear view of the field, was on the point, of ordering a party to rush forward with axes and beat down the formidable doors, when there came a blinding flash from the roof, something swished through the air, and a gust of heat met the assailants in the face. Bings dropped dead from his perch, and then, as if the scythe of the Destroyer had swung downward, and to right and left in quick succession, the close-packed mob was levelled, rank after rank, until the few survivors crept behind rocks for refuge.

Instantly the atmospheric broom swept up and down the canyon and across the mountain's flanks, and the marksmen fell in bunches like shaken grapes. Nine-tenths of the besiegers were destroyed within ten minutes after the first movement had been noticed on the roof. Those who survived owed their escape to the rocks which concealed them, and they lost no time in crawling off into neighboring chasms, and, as soon as

Garrett P. Serviss

they were beyond eye-shot from the mill, they fled with panic speed.

Then the towering form of Dr. Syx appeared at the door. Emerging without sign of fear or excitement, he picked his way among his fallen enemies, and, approaching the military guard-house, undid the fastening and set the imprisoned soldiers free.

"I think I am paying rather dear for my whistle," he said, with a characteristic sneer, to Captain Carter, the commander of the troop. "It seems that I must not only defend my own people and property when attacked by mob force, but must also come to the rescue of the soldiers whose pay-rolls are met from my pocket."

The captain made no reply, and Dr. Syx strode back to the works. When the released soldiers saw what had occurred their amazement had no bounds. It was necessary at once to dispose of the dead, and this was no easy undertaking for their small force. However, they accomplished it, and at the beginning of their work made a most surprising discovery.

"How's this, Jim?" said one of the men to his comrade, as they stooped to lift the nearest victim of Dr. Syx's withering fire. "What's this fellow got all over him?"

"Artemisium! 'pon my soul!" responded "Jim," staring at the body. "He's all coated over with it."

Immediately from all sides came similar exclamations. Every man who had fallen was covered with a film of the precious metal, as if he had been dipped into an electrolytic bath. Clothing seemed to have been charred, and the metallic atoms had penetrated the flesh of the victims. The rocks all round the battle-field were similarly veneered. "It looks to me," said Captain Carter, "as if old Syx had turned one of his spouts of artemisium into a hose-pipe and soaked 'em with it."

"That's it," chimed in a lieutenant, "that's exactly what he's done."

"Well," returned the captain, "if he can do that, I don't see what use he's got for us here."

"Probably he don't want to waste the stuff," said the lieutenant. "What do you suppose it cost him to plate this crowd?"

"I guess a month's pay for the whole troop wouldn't cover the expense. It's costly, but then - gracious! Wouldn't I have given something for the doctor's hose when I was a youngster campaigning in the Philippines in '99?"

The story of the marvellous way in which Dr. Syx defended his mill became the sensation of the world for many days. The hose-pipe theory, struck off on the spot by Captain Carter, seized the popular fancy, and was generally accepted without further question. There was an element of the ludicrous which robbed the tragedy of some of its horror. Moreover, no one could deny that Dr. Syx was well within his rights in defending himself by any means when so savagely attacked, and his triumphant success, no less than the ingenuity which was supposed to underlie it, placed him in an heroic light which he had not hitherto enjoyed.

As to the demagogues who were responsible for the

outbreak and its terrible consequences, they slunk out of the public eye, and the result of the battle at the mine seemed to have been a clearing up of the atmosphere, such as a thunderstorm effects at the close of a season of foul weather.

But now, little as men guessed it, the beginning of the end was close at hand.

IX

THE DETECTIVE OF SCIENCE

The morning of my arrival at Grand Teton station, on my return from the East, Andrew Hall met me with a warm greeting.

"I have been anxiously expecting you," he said, "for I have made some progress towards solving the great mystery. I have not yet reached a conclusion, but I hope soon to let you into the entire secret. In the meantime you can aid me with your companionship, if in no other way, for, since the defeat of the mob, this place has been mighty lonesome. The Grand Teton is a spot that people who have no particular business out here carefully avoid. I am on speaking terms with Dr. Syx, and occasionally, when there is a party to be shown around, I visit his works, and make the best possible use of my eyes. Captain Carter of the military is a capital fellow, and I like to hear his stories of the war in Luzon forty years ago, but I want somebody to whom I can occasionally confide things, and so you are as welcome as moonlight in harvest-time."

"Tell me something about that wonderful fight with the mob. Did you see it?"

"I did. I had got wind of what Bings intended to do

while I was down at Pocotello, and I hurried up here to warn the soldiers, but unfortunately I came too late. Finding the military cooped up in the guard-house and the mob masters of the situation, I kept out of sight on the side of the Teton, and watched the siege with my binocular. I think there was very little of the spectacle that I missed."

"What of the mysterious force that the doctor employed to sweep off the assailants?"

"Of course, Captain Carter's suggestion that Syx turned molten artemisium from his furnace into a hose-pipe and sprayed the enemy with it is ridiculous. But it is much easier to dismiss Carter's theory than to substitute a better one. I saw the doctor on the roof with a gang of black workmen, and I noticed the flash of polished metal turned rapidly this way and that, but there was some intervening obstacle which prevented me from getting a good view of the mechanism employed. It certainly bore no resemblance to a hose-pipe, or anything of that kind. No emanation was visible from the machine, but it was stupefying to see the mob melt down."

"How about the coating of the bodies with artemisium?"

"There you are back on the hose-pipe again," laughed Hall. "But, to tell you the truth, I'd rather be excused from expressing an opinion on that operation in wholesale electro-plating just at present. I've the ghost of an idea what it means, but let me test my theory a little before I formulate it. In the meanwhile, won't you take a stroll with me?"

"Certainly; nothing could please me better," I replied. "Which way shall we go?"

"To the top of the Grand Teton."

"What! are you seized with the mountain-climbing fever?"

"Not exactly, but I have a particular reason for wishing to take a look from that pinnacle."

"I suppose you know the real apex of the peak has never been trodden by man?"

"I do know it, but it is just that apex that I am determined to have under my feet for ten minutes. The failure of others is no argument for us."

"Just as you say," I rejoined. "But I suppose there is no indiscretion in asking whether this little climb has any relation to the mystery?"

"If it didn't have an important relation to the clearing up of that dark thing I wouldn't risk my neck in such an undertaking," was the reply.

Accordingly, the next morning we set out for the peak. All previous climbers, as we were aware, had attacked it from the west. That seemed the obvious thing to do, because the westward slopes of the mountain, while very steep, are less abrupt than those which face the rising sun. In fact, the eastern side of the Grand Teton appears to be absolutely unclimbable. But both Hall and I had had experience with rock climbing in the Alps and the Dolomites, and we knew that what looked like the hardest places sometimes turn out to be next to the easiest. Accordingly we decided - the more particularly because it would save time, but also because we yielded to the common desire to outdo our predecessors - to try to scale the giant right up his face.

We carried a very light but exceedingly strong rope, about five hundred feet long, wore nail-shod shoes, and had each a metal-pointed staff and a small hatchet in lieu of the regular mountaineer's axe. Advancing at first along the broken ridge between two gorges we gradually approached the steeper part of the Teton, where the cliffs looked so sheer and smooth that it seemed no wonder that nobody had ever tried to scale them. The air was deliciously clear and the sky wonderfully blue above the mountains, and the moon, a few days past its last quarter, was visible in the southwest, its pale crescent face slightly blued by the atmosphere, as it always appears when seen in daylight.

"Slow westering, a phantom sail -
The lonely soul of yesterday."

Behind us, somewhat north of east, lay the Syx works, with their black smoke rising almost vertically in the still air. Suddenly, as we stumbled along on the rough surface, something whizzed past my face and fell on the rock at my feet. I looked at the strange missile, that had come like a meteor out of open space, with astonishment.

It was a bird, a beautiful specimen of the scarlet tanagers, which I remembered the early explorers had found inhabiting the Teton canyons, their brilliant plumage borrowing splendor from contrast with the gloomy surroundings. It lay motionless, its outstretched wings having a curious shrivelled aspect, while the flaming color of the breast was half obliterated with smutty patches. Stooping to pick it up, I noticed a slight bronzing, which instantly recalled to my mind the peculiar appearance of the victims of the attack on the mine.

"Look here!" I called to Hall, who was several yards in advance. He turned, and I held up the bird by a wing.

"Where did you get that?" he asked.

"It fell at my feet a moment ago."

Hall glanced in a startled manner at the sky, and then down the slope of the mountain.

"Did you notice in what direction it was flying?" he asked.

"No, it dropped so close that it almost grazed my nose. I saw nothing of it until it made me blink."

"I have been heedless," muttered Hall under his breath. At the time I did not notice the singularity of his remark, my attention being absorbed in contemplating the unfortunate tanager.

"Look how its feathers are scorched," I said.

"I know it," Hall replied, without glancing at the bird.

"And it is covered with a film of artemisium," I added, a little piqued by his abstraction.

"I know that, too."

"See here, Hall," I exclaimed, "are you trying to make game of me?"

"Not at all, my dear fellow," he replied, dropping his cogitation. "Pray forgive me. But this is no new phenomenon to me. I have picked up birds in that condition on this mountain before. There is a terrible mystery here, but I am slowly letting light into it, and if we succeed in reaching the top of the peak I have good hope that the illumination will increase."

"Here now," he added a moment later, sitting down upon a rock and thrusting the blade of his penknife into a crevice, "what do you think of this?"

He held up a little nugget of pure artemisium, and then went on:

"You know that all this slope was swept as clean as a Dutch housewife's kitchen floor by the thousands of miners and prospectors who swarmed over it a year or two ago, and do you suppose they would have missed such a tidbit if it had been here then?"

"Dr. Syx must have been salting the mountain again," I suggested.

"Well," replied Hall, with a significant smile, "if the doctor hasn't salted it somebody else has, that's plain enough. But perhaps you would like to know precisely what I expect to find out when we get on the topknot of the Teton."

"I should certainly be delighted to learn the object of our journey," I said. "Of course, I'm only going along for company and for the fun of the thing; but you know you can count on me for substantial aid whenever you need it."

"It is because you are so willing to let me keep my own counsel," he rejoined, "and to wait for things to ripen before compelling me to disclose them, that I like to have you with me at critical times. Now, as to the object of this break-neck expedition, whose risks you understand as fully as I do, I need not assure you that it is of supreme importance to the success of my plans. In a word, I hope to be able to look down into a part of Dr. Syx's mill which, if I am not mistaken, no human eye except his and those of his most trustworthy helpers has ever been permitted to see. And if I see there what I fully expect to see, I shall have got a long step nearer to a great fortune."

"Good!" I cried. "*En avant*, then! We are losing time."

X

THE TOP OF THE GRAND TETON

The climbing soon became difficult, until at length we were going up hand over hand, taking advantage of crevices and knobs which an inexperienced eye would have regarded as incapable of affording a grip for the fingers or a support for the toes. Presently we arrived at the foot of a stupendous precipice, which was absolutely insurmountable by any ordinary method of ascent. Parts of it overhung, and everywhere the face of the rock was too free from irregularities to afford any footing, except to a fly.

"Now, to borrow the expression of old Bunyan, we are hard put to it," I remarked. "If you will go to the left I will take the right and see if there is any chance of getting up."

"I don't believe we could find any place easier than this," Hall replied, "and so up we go where we are."

"Have you a pair of wings concealed about you?" I asked, laughing at his folly.

"Well, something nearly as good," he responded, unstrapping his knapsack. He produced a silken bag, which he unfolded on the rock.

"A balloon!" I exclaimed. "But how are you going to inflate it?"

For reply Hall showed me a receptacle which, he said, contained liquid hydrogen, and which was furnished with a device for retarding the volatilization of the liquid so that it could be carried with little loss.

"You remember I have a small laboratory in the abandoned mine," he explained, "where we used to manufacture liquid air for blasting. This balloon I made for our present purpose. It will just suffice to carry up our rope, and a small but practically unbreakable grapple of hardened gold. I calculate to send the grapple to the top of the precipice with the balloon, and when it has obtained a firm hold in the riven rock there we can ascend, sailor fashion. You see the rope has knots, and I know your muscles are as trustworthy in such work as my own."

There was a slight breeze from the eastward, and the current of air slanting up the face of the peak assisted the balloon in mounting with its burden, and favored us by promptly swinging the little airship, with the grapple swaying beneath it, over the brow of the cliff into the atmospheric eddy above. As soon as we saw that the grapple was well over the edge we pulled upon the rope. The balloon instantly shot into view with the anchor dancing, but, under the influence of the wind, quickly returned to its former position behind the projecting brink. The grapple had failed to take hold.

"'Try, try again' must be our motto now," muttered Hall.

We tried several times with the same result, although

each time we slightly shifted our position. At last the grapple caught.

"Now, all together!" cried my companion, and simultaneously we threw our weight upon the slender rope. The anchor apparently did not give an inch.

"Let me go first," said Hall, pushing me aside as I caught the first knot above my head. "It's my device, and it's only fair that I should have the first try."

In a minute he was many feet up the wall, climbing swiftly hand over hand, but occasionally stopping and twisting his leg around the rope while he took breath.

"It's easier than I expected," he called down, when he had ascended about one hundred feet. "Here and there the rock offers a little hold for the knees."

I watched him, breathless with anxiety, and, as he got higher, my imagination pictured the little gold grapple, invisible above the brow of the precipice, with perhaps a single thin prong wedged into a crevice, and slowly ploughing its way towards the edge with each impulse of the climber, until but another pull was needed to set it flying! So vivid was my fancy that I tried to banish it by noticing that a certain knot in the rope remained just at the level of my eyes, where it had been from the start. Hall was now fully two hundred feet above the ledge on which I stood, and was rapidly nearing the top of the precipice. In a minute more he would be safe.

Suddenly he shouted, and, glancing up with a leap of the heart, I saw that he was falling! He kept his face to the rock, and came down feet foremost. It would be useless to attempt any description of my feelings; I would not go through that experience again for the price of a battleship. Yet it lasted less than a second. He had dropped not more than ten feet when the fall was arrested.

"All right!" he called, cheerily. "No harm done! It was only a slip."

But what a slip! If the balloon had not carried the anchor several yards back from the edge it would have had no opportunity to catch another hold as it shot forward. And how could we know that the second hold would prove more secure than the first? Hall did not hesitate, however, for one instant. Up he went again. But, in fact, his best chance was in going up, for he was within four yards of the top when the mishap occurred. With a sigh of relief I saw him at last throw his arm over the verge and then wriggle his body upon the ledge. A few seconds later he was lying on his stomach, with his face over the edge, looking down at me.

"Come on!" he shouted. "It's all right."

When I had pulled myself over the brink at his side I grasped his hand and pressed it without a word. We understood one another.

"It was pretty close to a miracle," he remarked at last. "Look at this."

The rock over which the grapple had slipped was deeply scored by the unyielding point of the metal, and exactly at the verge of the precipice the prong had wedged itself into a narrow crack, so firmly that we had to chip away the stone in order to release it. If it had slipped a single inch farther before taking hold it would have been all over with my friend.

Such experiences shake the strongest nerves, and we sat on the shelf we had attained for fully a quarter of an hour before we ventured to attack the next precipice which hung beetling directly above us. It was not as lofty as the one we had just ascended, but it impended to such a degree that we saw we should have to climb our rope while it swung free in the air!

Luckily we had little difficulty in getting a grip for the prongs, and we took every precaution to test the security of the anchorage, not only putting our combined weight repeatedly upon the rope, but flipping and jerking it with all our strength. The grapple resisted every effort to dislodge it, and finally I started up, insisting on my turn as leader.

The height I had to ascend did not exceed one hundred feet, but that is a very great distance to climb on a swinging rope, without a wall within reach to assist by its friction and occasional friendly projections. In a little while my movements, together with the effect of the slight wind, had imparted a most distressing oscillation to the rope. This sometimes carried me with a nerve-shaking bang against a prominent point of the precipice, where I would dislodge loose fragments that kept Hall dodging for his life, and then I would swing out, apparently beyond the brow of the cliff below, so that, as I involuntarily glanced downward, I seemed to be hanging in free space, while the steep mountainside, looking ten times steeper than it really was, resembled the vertical wall of an absolutely bottomless abyss, as if I were suspended over the edge of the world.

I avoided thinking of what the grapple might be about, and in my haste to get through with the awful experience I worked myself fairly out of breath, so that, when at last I reached the rounded brow of the cliff, I had to stop and cling there for fully a minute before I could summon strength enough to lift myself over it.

When I was assured that the grapple was still securely fastened I signalled to Hall, and he soon stood at my side, exclaiming, as he wiped the perspiration from his face:

"I think I'll try wings next time!"

But our difficulties had only begun. As we had foreseen, it was a case of Alp above Alp, to the very limit of human strength and patience. However, it would have been impossible to go back. In order to descend the two precipices we had surmounted it would have been necessary to leave our life-lines clinging to the rocks, and we had not rope enough to do that. If we could not reach the top we were lost.

Having refreshed ourselves with a bite to eat and a little stimulant, we resumed the climb. After several hours of the most exhausting work I have ever performed we pulled our weary limbs upon the narrow ridge, but a few square yards in area, which constitutes the apex of the Grand Teton. A little below, on the opposite side of a steep-walled gap which divides the top of the mountain into two parts, we saw the singular enclosure of stones which the early white explorers found there, and which they ascribed to the Indians, although nobody has ever known who built it or what purpose it served.

The view was, of course, superb, but while I was admiring it in all its wonderful extent and variety, Hall, who had immediately pulled out his binocular, was busy inspecting the Syx works, the top of whose great tufted smoke column was thousands of feet beneath our level. Jackson's Lake, Jenny's Lake, Leigh's Lake, and several lakelets glittered in the sunlight amid the pale grays and greens of Jackson's Hole, while many a bending reach of the Snake River shone amid the wastes of sage-brush and rock.

"There!" suddenly exclaimed Hall, "I thought I should find it."

"What?"

"Take a look through my glass at the roof of Syx's mill. Look just in the centre."

"Why, it's open in the middle!" I cried as soon as I had put the glass to my eyes. "There's a big circular hole in the centre of the roof,"

"Look inside! Look inside!" repeated Hall, impatiently.

"I see nothing there except something bright."

"Do you call it nothing because it is bright?"

"Well, no," I replied, laughing. "What I mean is that I see nothing that I can make anything of except a shining object, and all I can make of that is that it is bright."

"You've been in the Syx works many times, haven't you?"

"Yes."

"Did you ever see the opening in the roof?"

"Never."

"Did you ever hear of it?"

"Never."

"Then Dr. Syx doesn't show his visitors everything that is to be seen."

"Evidently not since, as we know, he concealed the double tunnel and the room under the furnace."

"Dr. Syx has concealed a bigger secret than that," Hall responded, "and the Grand Teton has helped me to a glimpse of it."

For several minutes my friend was absorbed in thought. Then he broke out:

"I tell you he's the most wonderful man in the world!"

"Who, Dr. Syx? Well, I've long thought that."

"Yes, but I mean in a different way from what you are thinking of. Do you remember my asking you once if you believed in alchemy?"

"I remember being greatly surprised by your question to that effect."

"Well, now," said Hall, rubbing his hands with a satisfied air, while his eyes glanced keen and bright with the reflection of some passing thought, "Max Syx is greater than any alchemist that ever lived. If those old fellows in the dark ages had accomplished everything they set out to do, they would have been of no more consequence in comparison with our black-browed friend down yonder than - than my head is of consequence in comparison with the moon."

"I fear you flatter the man in the moon," was my laughing reply.

"No, I don't," returned Hall, "and some day you'll admit it."

"Well, what about that something that shines down there? You seem to see more in it than I can."

But my companion had fallen into a reverie and didn't hear my question. He was gazing abstractedly at the faint image of the waning moon, now nearing the distant mountain-top over in Idaho. Presently his mind seemed to return to the old magnet, and he whirled about and glanced down at the Syx mill. The column of smoke was diminishing in volume, an indication that the engine was about to enjoy one of its periodical rests. The irregularity of these stoppages had always been a subject of remark among practical engineers. The hours of labor were exceedingly erratic, but the engine had never been known to work at night, except on one occasion, and then only for a few minutes, when it was suddenly stopped on account of a fire.

Just as Hall resumed his inspection two huge quarter spheres, which had been resting wide apart on the roof, moved towards one another until their arched sections met over the circular aperture which they covered like the dome of an observatory.

"I expected it," Hall remarked. "But come, it is mid-afternoon, and we shall need all of our time to get safely down before the light fades."

As I have already explained, it would not have been possible for us to return the way we came. We determined to descend the comparatively easy western slopes of the peak, and pass the night on that side of the mountain. Letting ourselves down with the rope into the hollow way that divides the summit of the Teton into two pinnacles, we had no difficulty in descending by the route followed by all previous climbers. The weather was fine, and, having found good shelter among the rocks, we passed the night in comfort. The next day we succeeded in swinging round upon the eastern flank of the Teton, below the more formidable cliffs, and, just at nightfall, we arrived at the station. As we passed the Syx mine the doctor himself confronted us. There was a very displeasing look on his dark countenance, and his sneer was strongly marked.

"So you have been on top of the Teton?" he said.

"Yes," replied Hall, very blandly, "and if you have a taste for that sort of thing I should advise you to go up. The view is immense, as fine as the best in the Alps."

"Pretty ingenious plan, that balloon of yours," continued the doctor, still looking black.

"Thank you," Hall replied, more suavely than ever. "I've been planning that a long time. You probably don't know that mountaineering used to be my chief amusement."

The doctor turned away without pursuing the conversation.

"I could kick myself," Hall muttered as soon as Dr. Syx was out of earshot. "If my absurd wish to outdo others had not blinded me, I should have known that he would see us going up this side of the peak, particularly with the balloon to give us away. However, what's done can't be undone. He may not really suspect the truth, and if he does he can't help himself, even though he is the richest man in the world."

XI

STRANGE FATE OF A KITE

"Are you ready for another tramp?" was Andrew Hall's greeting when we met early on the morning following our return from the peak.

"Certainly I am. What is your programme for to-day?"

"I wish to test the flying qualities of a kite which I have constructed since our return last night."

"You don't allow the calls of sleep to interfere very much with your activity."

"I haven't much time for sleep just now," replied Hall, without smiling. "The kite test will carry us up the flanks of the Teton, but I am not going to try for the top this time. If you will come along I'll ask you to help me by carrying and operating a light transit I shall carry another myself. I am desirous to get the elevation that the kite attains and certain other data that will be of use to me. We will make a detour towards the south, for I don't want old Syx's suspicions to be prodded any more."

"What interest can he have in your kite-flying?"

"The same interest that a burglar has in the rap of a policeman's night-stick."

"Then your experiment to-day has some connection with the solution of the great mystery?"

"My dear fellow," said Hall, laying his hand on my shoulder, "until I see the end of that mystery I shall think of nothing else."

In a few hours we were clambering over the broken rocks on the south-eastern flank of the Teton at an elevation of about three thousand feet above the level of Jackson's Hole. Finally Hall paused and began to put his kite together. It was a small box-shaped affair, very light in construction, with paper sides.

"In order to diminish the chances of Dr. Syx noticing what we are about," he said, as he worked away, "I have covered the kite with sky-blue paper. This, together with distance, will probably insure us against his notice."

In a few minutes the kite was ready. Having ascertained the direction of the wind with much attention, he stationed me with my transit on a commanding rock, and sought another post for himself at a distance of two hundred yards, which he carefully measured with a gold tape. My instructions were to keep the telescope on the kite as soon as it had attained a considerable height, and to note the angle of elevation and the horizontal angle with the base line joining our points of observation.

"Be particularly careful," was Hall's injunction, "and if anything happens to the kite by all means note the angles at that instant."

As soon as we had fixed our stations Hall began to pay out the string, and the kite rose very swiftly. As it sped away into the blue it was soon practically invisible to the naked eye, although the telescope of the transit enabled me to follow it with ease.

Glancing across now and then at my companion, I noticed that he was having considerable difficulty in, at the same time, managing the kite and manipulating his transit. But as the kite continued to rise and steadied in position his task became easier, until at length he ceased to remove his eye from the telescope while holding the string with outstretched hand.

"Don't lose sight of it now for an instant!" he shouted.

For at least half an hour he continued to manipulate the string, sending the kite now high towards the zenith with a sudden pull, and then letting it drift off. It seemed at last to become almost a fixed point. Very slowly the angles changed, when, suddenly, there was a flash, and to my amazement I saw the paper of the kite shrivel and disappear in a momentary flame, and then the bare sticks came tumbling out of the sky.

"Did you get the angles?" yelled Hall, excitedly.

"Yes; the telescope is yet pointed on the spot where the kite disappeared."

"Read them off," he called, "and then get your angle with the Syx works."

"All right," I replied, doing as he had requested, and

noticing at the same time that he was in the act of putting his watch in his pocket. "Is there anything else?" I asked.

"No, that will do, thank you."

Hall came running over, his face beaming, and with the air of a man who has just hooked a particularly cunning old trout.

"Ah!" he exclaimed, "this has been a great success! I could almost dispense with the calculation, but it is best to be sure."

"What are you about, anyhow?" I asked, "and what was it that happened to the kite?"

"Don't interrupt me just now, please," was the only reply I received.

Thereupon my friend sat down on a rock, pulled out a pad of paper, noted the angles which I had read on the transit, and fell to figuring with feverish haste. In the course of his work he consulted a pocket almanac, then glanced up at the sky, muttered approvingly, and finally leaped to his feet with a half-suppressed "Hurrah!" If I had not known him so well I should have thought that he had gone daft.

"Will you kindly tell me," I asked, "how you managed to set the kite afire?"

Hall laughed heartily. "You though it was a trick, did you?" said he. "Well, it was no trick, but a very beautiful demonstration. You surely haven't forgotten the scarlet tanager that gave you such a surprise the day before yesterday."

"Do you mean" I exclaimed, startled at the suggestion, "that the fate of the bird had any connection with the accident to your kite?"

"Accident isn't precisely the right word," replied Hall. "The two things are as intimately related as own brothers. If you should care to hunt up the kite sticks, you would find that they, too, are now artemisium plated."

"This is getting too deep for me," was all that I could say.

"I am not absolutely confident that I have touched bottom myself," said Hall, "but I'm going to make another dive, and if I don't bring up treasures greater than Vanderdecken found at the bottom of the sea, then Dr. Syx is even a more wonderful human mystery than I have thought him to be."

"What do you propose to do next?"

"To shake the dust of the Grand Teton from my shoes and go to San Francisco, where I have an extensive laboratory."

"So you are going to try a little alchemy yourself, are you?"

"Perhaps; who knows? At any rate, my good friend, I am forever indebted to you for your assistance, and even more for your discretion, and if I succeed you shall be the first person in the world to hear the news."

XII

BETTER THAN ALCHEMY

I come now to a part of my narrative which would have been deemed altogether incredible in those closing years of the nineteenth century that witnessed the first steps towards the solution of the deepest mysteries of the ether, although men even then held in their hands, without knowing it, powers which, after they had been mastered and before use had made them familiar, seemed no less than godlike.

For six months after Hall's departure for San Francisco I heard nothing from him. Notwithstanding my intense desire to know what he was doing, I did not seek to disturb him in his retirement. In the meantime things ran on as usual in the world, only a ripple being caused by renewed discoveries of small nuggets of artemisium on the Tetons, a fact which recalled to my mind the remark of my friend when he dislodged a flake of the metal from a crevice during our ascent of the peak. At last one day I received this telegram at my office in New York:

"SAN FRANCISCO, May 16, 1940.

"Come at once. The mystery is solved.

"(Signed) HALL."

As soon as I could pack a grip I was flying westward one hundred miles an hour. On reaching San Francisco, which had made enormous strides since the opening of the twentieth century, owing to the extension of our Oriental possessions, and which already ranked with New York and Chicago among the financial capitals of the world, I hastened to Hall's laboratory. He was there expecting me, and, after a hearty greeting, during which his elation over his success was manifest, he said:

"I am compelled to ask you to make a little journey. I found it impossible to secure the necessary privacy here, and, before opening my experiments, I selected a site for a new laboratory in an unfrequented spot among the mountains this side of Lake Tahoe. You will be the first man, with the exception of my two devoted assistants, to see my apparatus, and you shall share the sensation of the critical experiment."

"Then you have not yet completed your solution of the secret?"

"Yes, I have; for I am as certain of the result as if I had seen it, but I thought you were entitled to be in with me at the death."

From the nearest railway station we took horses to the laboratory, which occupied a secluded but most beautiful site at an elevation of about six thousand feet above sea-level. With considerable surprise I noticed a building surmounted with a dome, recalling what we had seen from the Grand Teton on the roof of Dr. Syx's mill. Hall, observing my look, smiled significantly, but said nothing. The laboratory proper occupied a smaller building adjoining the domed structure. Hall led the way into an apartment having but a single door and illuminated by a skylight.

"This is my sanctum sanctorum," he said, "and you are the first outsider to enter it. Seat yourself comfortably while I proceed to unveil a little corner of the artemisium mystery."

Near one end of the room, which was about thirty feet in length, was a table, on which lay a glass tube about two inches in diameter and thirty inches long. In the farther end of the tube gleamed a lump of yellow metal, which I took to be gold. Hall and I were seated near another table about twenty-five feet distant from the tube, and on this table was an apparatus furnished with a concave mirror, whose optical axis was directed towards the tube. It occurred to me at once that this apparatus would be suitable for experimenting with electric waves. Wires ran from it to the floor, and in the cellar beneath was audible the beating of an engine. My companion made an adjustment or two, and then remarked:

"Now, keep your eyes on the lump of gold in the farther end of the tube yonder. The tube is exhausted of air, and I am about to concentrate upon the gold an intense electric influence, which will have the effect of making it a kind of kathode pole. I only use this term for the sake of illustration. You will recall that as long ago as the days of Crookes it was known that a kathode in an exhausted tube would project particles, or atoms, of its substance away in straight lines. Now watch!"

I fixed my attention upon the gold, and presently saw it

enveloped in a most beautiful violet light. This grew more intense, until, at times, it was blinding, while, at the same moment, the interior of the tube seemed to have become charged with a luminous vapor of a delicate pinkish hue.

"Watch! Watch!" said Hall. "Look at the nearer end of the tube!"

"Why, it is becoming coated with gold!" I exclaimed.

He smiled, but made no reply. Still the strange process continued. The pink vapor became so dense that the lump of gold was no longer visible, although the eye of violet light glared piercingly through the colored fog. Every second the deposit of metal, shining like a mirror, increased, until suddenly there came a curious whistling sound. Hall, who had been adjusting the mirror, jerked away his hand and gave it a flip, as if hot water had spattered it, and then the light in the tube quickly died away, the vapor escaped, filling the room with a peculiar stimulating odor, and I perceived that the end of the glass tube had been melted through, and the molten gold was slowly dripping from it.

"I carried it a little too far," said Hall, ruefully rubbing the back of his hand, "and when the glass gave way under the atomic bombardment a few atoms of gold visited my bones. But there is no harm done. You observed that the instant the air reached the kathode, as I for convenience call the electrified mass of gold, the action ceased."

"But your anode, to continue your simile," I said, "is constantly exposed to the air."

Garrett P. Serviss

"True," he replied, "but in the first place, of course, this is not really an anode, just as the other is not actually a kathode. As science advances we are compelled, for a time, to use old terms in a new sense until a fresh nomenclature can be invented. But we are now dealing with a form of electric action more subtle in its effects than any at present described in the text-books and the transactions of learned societies. I have not yet even attempted to work out the theory of it. I am only concerned with its facts."

"But wonderful as the exhibition you have given is, I do not see," I said, "how it concerns Dr. Syx and his artemisium."

"Listen," replied Hall, settling back in his chair after disconnecting his apparatus. "You no doubt have been told how one night the Syx engine was heard working for a few minutes, the first and only night work it was ever known to have done, and how, hardly had it started up when a fire broke out in the mill, and the engine was instantly stopped. Now there is a very remarkable story connected with that, and it will show you how I got my first clew to the mystery, although it was rather a mere suspicion than a clew, for at first I could make nothing out of it. The alleged fire occurred about a fortnight after our discovery of the double tunnel. My mind was then full of suspicions concerning Syx, because I thought that a man who would fool people with one hand was not likely to deal fairly with the other.

"It was a glorious night, with a full moon, whose face was so clear in the limpid air that, having found a snug place at the foot of a yellow-pine-tree, where the ground was carpeted with odoriferous needles, I lay on my back and renewed my early acquaintance with the romantically named mountains and 'seas' of the Lunar globe. With my binocular I could trace those long white streaks which radiate from the crater ring, called 'Tycho,' and run hundreds of miles in all directions over the moon. As I gazed at these singular objects I recalled the various theories which astronomers, puzzled by their enigmatical aspect, have offered to a more or less confiding public concerning them.

"In the midst of my meditation and moon gazing I was startled by hearing the engine in the Syx works suddenly begin to run. Immediately a queer light, shaped like the beam of a ship's searchlight, but reddish in color, rose high in the moonlit heavens above the mill. It did not last more than a minute or two, for almost instantly the engine was stopped, and with its stoppage the light faded and soon disappeared. The next day Dr. Syx gave it out that on starting up his engine in the night something had caught fire, which compelled him immediately to shut down again. The few who had seen the light, with the exception of your humble servant, accepted the doctor's explanation without a question. But I knew there had been no fire, and Syx's anxiety to spread the lie led me to believe that he had narrowly escaped giving away a vital secret. I said nothing about my suspicions, but upon inquiry I found out that an extra and pressing order for metal had arrived from the Austrian government the very day of the pretended fire, and I drew the inference that Syx, in his haste to fill the order - his supply having been drawn low - had started to work, contrary to his custom, at night, and had immediately found reason to repent his rashness. Of course, I connected the strange light with this sudden change of mind.

Garrett P. Serviss

"My suspicion having been thus stimulated, and having been directed in a certain way, I began, from that moment to notice closely the hours during which the engine labored. At night it was always quiet, except on that one brief occasion. Sometimes it began early in the morning and stopped about noon. At other times the work was done entirely in the afternoon, beginning sometimes as late as three or four o'clock, and ceasing invariably at sundown. Then again it would start at sunrise and continue the whole day through.

"For a long time I was unable to account for these eccentricities, and the problem was not rendered much clearer, although a startling suggestiveness was added to it, when, at length, I noticed that the periods of activity of the engine had a definite relation to the age of the moon. Then I discovered, with the aid of an almanac, that I could predict the hours when the engine would be busy. At the time of new moon it worked all day; at full moon, it was idle; between full moon and last quarter, it labored in the forenoon, the length of its working hours increasing as the quarter was approached; between last quarter and new moon, the hours of work lengthened, until, as I have said, at new moon they lasted all day; between new moon and first quarter, work began later and later in the forenoon as the quarter was approached, and between first quarter and full moon the laboring hours rapidly shortened, being confined to the latter part of the afternoon, until at full moon complete silence reigned in the mill."

"Well! well!" I broke in, greatly astonished by Hall's singular recital, "you must have thought Dr. Syx was a cross between an alchemist and an astrologer."

"Note this," said Hall, disregarding my interruption,

"the hours when the engine worked were invariably the hours during which the moon was above the horizon!"

"What did you infer from that?" "Of course, I inferred that the moon was directly concerned in the mystery; but how? That bothered me for a long time, but a little light broke into my mind when I picked up, on the mountain-side, a dead bird, whose scorched feathers were bronzed with artemisium, and sometime later another similar victim of a mysterious form of death. Then came the attack on the mine and its tragic finish. I have already told you what I observed on that occasion. But, instead of helping to clear up the mystery, it rather complicated it for a time. At length, however, I reasoned my way partly out of the difficulty. Certain things which I had noticed in the Syx mill convinced me that there was a part of the building whose existence no visitor suspected, and, putting one thing with another, I inferred that the roof must be open above that secret part of the structure, and that if I could get upon a sufficiently elevated place I could see something of what was hidden there.

"At this point in the investigation I proposed to you the trip to the top of the Teton, the result of which you remember. I had calculated the angles with great care, and I felt certain that from the apex of the mountain I should be able to get a view into the concealed chamber, and into just that side of it which I wished particularly to inspect. You remember that I called your attention to a shining object underneath the circular opening in the roof. You could not make out what it was, but I saw enough to convince me that it was a gigantic parabolic mirror. I'll show you a smaller one of the same kind presently.

"Now, at last, I began to perceive the real truth, but it was so wildly incredible, so infinitely remote from all human experience, that I hardly ventured to formulate it, even in my own secret mind. But I was bound to see the thing through to the end. It occurred to me that I could prove the accuracy of my theory with the aid of a kite. You were kind enough to lend your assistance in that experiment, and it gave me irrefragable evidence of the existence of a shaft of flying atoms extending in a direct line between Dr. Syx's pretended mine and the moon!"

"Hall!" I exclaimed, "you are mad!" My friend smiled good-naturedly, and went on with his story.

"The instant the kite shrivelled and disappeared I understood why the works were idle when the moon was not above the horizon, why birds flying across that fatal beam fell dead upon the rocks, and whence the terrible master of that mysterious mill derived the power of destruction that could wither an army as the Assyrian host in Byron's poem

"Melted like snow in the glance of the Lord."

"But how did Dr. Syx turn the flying atoms against his enemies?" I asked.

"In a very simple manner. He had a mirror mounted so that it could be turned in any direction, and would shunt the stream of metallic atoms, heated by their friction with the air, towards any desired point. When the attack came he raised this machine above the level of the roof and swept the mob to a lustrous, if expensive, death."

"And the light at night -"

"Was the shining of the heated atoms, not luminous enough to be visible in broad day, for which reason the engine never worked at night, and the stream of volatilized artemisium was never set flowing at full moon, when the lunar globe is above the horizon only during the hours of darkness."

"I see," I said, "whence came the nuggets on the mountain. Some of the atoms, owing to the resistance of the air, fell short and settled in the form of impalpable dust until the winds and rains collected and compacted them in the cracks and crevices of the rocks."

"That was it, of course."

"And now," I added, my amazement at the success of Hall's experiments and the accuracy of his deductions increasing every moment, "do you say that you have also discovered the means employed by Dr. Syx to obtain artemisium from the moon?"

"Not only that," replied my friend, "but within the next few minutes I shall have the pleasure of presenting to you a button of moon metal, fresh from the veins of Artemis herself."

XIII

THE LOOTING OF THE MOON

I shall spare the reader a recital of the tireless efforts, continuing through many almost sleepless weeks, whereby Andrew Hall obtained his clew to Dr. Syx's method. It was manifest from the beginning that the agent concerned must be some form of etheric, or so-called electric, energy; but how to set it in operation was the problem. Finally he hit upon the apparatus for his initial experiments which I have already described.

"Recurring to what had been done more than half a century ago by Hertz, when he concentrated electric waves upon a focal point by means of a concave mirror," said Hall, "I saw that the key I wanted lay in an extension of these experiments. At last I found that I could transform the energy of an engine into undulations of the ether, which, when they had been concentrated upon a metallic object, like a chunk of gold, imparted to it an intense charge of an apparently electric nature. Upon thus charging a metallic body enclosed in a vacuum, I observed that the energy imparted to it possessed the remarkable power of disrupting its atoms and projecting them off in straight lines, very much as occurs with a kathode in a Crookes's tube. But - and this was of supreme importance - I found that the line of projection was directly towards the apparatus from which the impulse producing the charge had come. In other words, I could produce two poles between which a marvellous interaction occurred. My transformer, with its concentrating mirror, acted as one pole, from which energy was transferred to the other pole, and that other pole immediately flung off atoms of its own substance in the direction of the transformer. But these atoms were stopped by the glass wall of the vacuum tube; and when I tried the experiment with the metal removed from the vacuum, and surrounded with air, it failed utterly.

"This at first completely discouraged me, until I suddenly remembered that the moon is in a vacuum, the great vacuum of interplanetary space, and that it possesses no perceptible atmosphere of its own. At this a great light broke around me, and I shouted 'Eureka!' Without hesitation I constructed a transformer of great power, furnished with a large parabolic mirror to transmit the waves in parallel lines, erected the machinery and buildings here, and when all was ready for the final experiment I telegraphed for you." Prepared by these explanations I was all on fire to see the thing tried. Hall was no less eager, and, calling in his two faithful assistants to make the final adjustments, he led the way into what he facetiously named "the lunar chamber."

"If we fail," he remarked with a smile that had an element of worriment in it, "it will become the 'lunatic chamber' - but no danger of that. You observe this polished silver knob, supported by a metallic rod curved over at the top like a crane. That constitutes the pole from which I propose to transmit the energy to the moon, and upon which I expect the storm of atoms to be centred by reflection from the mirror at whose focus it is placed."

"One moment," I said. "Am I to understand that you think that the moon is a solid mass of artemisium, and that no matter where your radiant force strikes it a 'kathodic pole' will be formed there from which atoms will be projected to the earth?"

"No," said Hall, "I must carefully choose the point on the lunar surface where to operate. But that will present no difficulty. I made up my mind as soon as I had penetrated Syx's secret that he obtained the metal from those mystic white streaks which radiate from Tycho, and which have puzzled the astronomers ever since the invention of telescopes. I now believe those streaks to be composed of immense veins of the metal that Syx has most appropriately named artemisium, which you, of course, recognize as being derived from the name of the Greek goddess of the moon, Artemis, whom the Romans called Diana. But now to work!"

It was less than a day past the time of new moon, and the earth's satellite was too near the sun to be visible in broad daylight. Accordingly, the mirror had to be directed by means of knowledge of the moon's place in the sky. Driven by accurate clockwork, it could be depended upon to retain the proper direction when once set.

With breathless interest I watched the proceedings of my friend and his assistants. The strain upon the nerves of all of us was such as could not have been borne for many hours at a stretch. When everything had been adjusted to his satisfaction, Hall stepped back, not without betraying his excitement in flushed cheeks and flashing eyes, and pressed a lever. The powerful engine underneath the floor instantly responded. The experiment was begun.

"I have set it upon a point about a hundred miles north of Tycho, where the Yerkes photographs show a great abundance of the white substance," said Hall.

Then we waited. A minute elapsed. A bird, fluttering in the opening above, for a second or two, wrenched our strained nerves. Hall's face turned pale.

"They had better keep away from here," he whispered, with a ghastly smile.

Two minutes! I could hear the beating of my heart. The engine shook the floor.

Three minutes! Hall's face was wet with perspiration. The bird blundered in and startled us again.

Four minutes! We were like statues, with all eyes fixed on the polished ball of silver, which shone in the brilliant light concentrated upon it by the mirror.

Five minutes! The shining ball had become a confused blue, and I violently winked to clear my vision.

"At last! Thank God! Look! There it is!"

It was Hall who spoke, trembling like an aspen. The silver knob had changed color. What seemed a miniature rainbow surrounded it, with concentric circles of blinding brilliance.

Then something dropped flashing into an earthen dish

set beneath the ball! Another glittering drop followed, and, at a shorter interval, another!

Almost before a word could be uttered the drops had coalesced and become a tiny stream, which, as it fell, twisted itself into a bright spiral, gleaming with a hundred shifting hues, and forming on the bottom of the dish a glowing, interlacing maze of viscid rings and circlets, which turned and twined about and over one another, until they had blended and settled into a button-shaped mass of hot metallic jelly. Hall snatched the dish away, and placed another in its stead.

"This will be about right for a watch charm when it cools," he said, with a return of his customary self-command. "I promised you the first specimen. I'll catch another for myself."

"But can it be possible that we are not dreaming?" I exclaimed. "Do you really believe that this comes from the moon?"

"Just as surely as rain comes from the clouds," cried Hall, with all his old impatience. "Haven't I just showed you the whole process?"

"Then I congratulate you. You will be as rich as Dr. Syx."

"Perhaps," was the unperturbed reply, "but not until I have enlarged my apparatus. At present I shall hardly do more than supply mementoes to my friends. But since the principle is established, the rest is mere detail."

Six weeks later the financial centres of the earth were

shaken by the news that a new supply of artemisium was being marketed from a mill which had been secretly opened in the Sierras of California. For a time there was almost a panic. If Hall had chosen to do so, he might have precipitated serious trouble. But he immediately entered into negotiations with government representatives, and the inevitable result was that, to preserve the monetary system of the world from upheaval, Dr. Syx had to consent that Hall's mill should share equally with his in the production of artemisium. During the negotiations the doctor paid a visit to Hall's establishment. The meeting between them was most dramatic. Syx tried to blast his rival with a glance, but knowledge is power, and my friend faced his mysterious antagonist, whose deepest secrets he had penetrated, with an unflinching eye. It was remarked that Dr. Syx became a changed man from that moment. His masterful air seemed to have deserted him, and it was with something resembling humility that he assented to the arrangement which required him to share his enormous gains with his conqueror.

Of course, Hall's success led to an immediate recrudescence of the efforts to extract artemisium from the Syx ore, and, equally of course, every such attempt failed. Hall, while keeping his own secret, did all he could to discourage the experiments, but they naturally believed that he must have made the very discovery which was the subject of their dreams, and he could not, without betraying himself, and upsetting the finances of the planet, directly undeceive them. The consequence was that fortunes were wasted in hopeless experimentation, and, with Hall's achievement dazzling their eyes, the deluded fortune-seekers kept on in the face of endless disappointments and disaster.

Garrett P. Serviss

And presently there came another tragedy. The Syx mill was blown up! The accident - although many people refused to regard it as an accident, and asserted that the doctor himself, in his chagrin, had applied the match - the explosion, then, occurred about sundown, and its effects were awful. The great works, with everything pertaining to them, and every rail that they contained, were blown to atoms. They disappeared as if they had never existed. Even the twin tunnels were involved in the ruin, a vast cavity being left in the mountain-side where Syx's ten acres had been. The force of the explosion was so great that the shattered rock was reduced to dust. To this fact was owing the escape of the troops camped near. While the mountain was shaken to its core, and enormous parapets of living rock were hurled down the precipices of the Teton, no missiles of appreciable size traversed the air, and not a man at the camp was injured. But Jackson's Hole, filled with red dust, looked for days afterwards like the mouth of a tremendous volcano just after an eruption. Dr. Syx had been seen entering the mill a few minutes before the catastrophe by a sentinel who was stationed about a quarter of a mile away, and who, although he was felled like an ox by the shock, and had his eyes, ears, and nostrils filled with flying dust, miraculously escaped with his life.

After this a new arrangement was made whereby Andrew Hall became the sole producer of artemisium, and his wealth began to mount by leaps of millions towards the starry heights of the billions.

About a year after the explosion of the Syx mill a strange rumor got about. It came first from Budapest, in Hungary, where it was averred several persons of credibility had seen Dr. Max Syx. Millions had been familiar with his face and his personal peculiarities, through actually meeting him, as well as through photographs and descriptions, and, unless there was an intention to deceive, it did not seem possible that a mistake could be made in identification. There surely never was another man who looked just like Dr. Syx. And, besides, was it not demonstrable that he must have perished in the awful destruction of his mill?

Soon after came a report that Dr. Syx had been seen again; this time at Ekaterinburg, in the Urals. Next he was said to have paid a visit to Batang, in the mountainous district of southwestern China, and finally, according to rumor, he was seen in Sicily, at Nicolosi, among the volcanic pimples on the southern slope of Mount Etna.

Next followed something of more curious and even startling interest. A chemist at Budapest, where the first rumors of Syx's reappearance had placed the mysterious doctor, announced that he could produce artemisium, and proved it, although he kept his process secret. Hardly had the sensation caused by this news partially subsided when a similar report arrived from Ekaterinburg; then another from Batang; after that a fourth from Nicolosi!

Nobody could fail to notice the coincidence; wherever the doctor - or was it his ghost? - appeared, there, shortly afterwards, somebody discovered the much-sought secret.

After this Syx's apparitions rapidly increased in frequency, followed in each instance by the announce-ment of another productive artemisium mill. He appeared in Germany, Italy, France, England, and finally at many places in the United States.

"It is the old doctor's revenge," said Hall to me one day, trying to smile, although the matter was too serious to be taken humorously. "Yes, it is his revenge, and I must admit that it is complete. The price of artemisium has fallen one-half within six months. All the efforts we have made to hold back the flood have proved useless. The secret itself is becoming public property. We shall inevitably be overwhelmed with artemisium, just as we were with gold, and the last condition of the financial world will be worse than the first."

My friend's gloomy prognostications came near being fulfilled to the letter. Ten thousand artemisium mills shot their etheric rays upon the moon, and our unfortunate satellite's metal ribs were stripped by atomic force. Some of the great white rays that had been one of the telescopic wonders of the lunar landscapes disappeared, and the face of the moon, which had remained unchanged before the eyes of the children of Adam from the beginning of their race, now looked as if the blast of a furnace had swept it. At night, on the moonward side, the earth was studded with brilliant spikes, all pointed at the heart of its child in the sky.

But the looting of the moon brought disaster to the robber planet. So mad were the efforts to get the precious metal that the surface of our globe was fairly showered with it, productive fields were, in some cases, almost smothered under a metallic coating, the air was filled with shining dust, until finally famine and pestilence joined hands with financial disaster to punish the grasping world.

Then, at last, the various governments took effective measures to protect themselves and their people. Another combined effort resulted in an international agreement whereby the production of the precious moon metal was once more rigidly controlled. But the existence of a monopoly, such as Dr. Syx had so long enjoyed, and in the enjoyment of which Andrew Hall had for a brief period succeeded him, was henceforth rendered impossible.

XIV

THE LAST OF DR. SYX

Many years after the events last recorded I sat, at the close of a brilliant autumn day, side by side with my old friend Andrew Hall, on a broad, vine-shaded piazza which faced the east, where the full moon was just rising above the rim of the Sierra, and replacing the rosy counter-glow of sunset with its silvery radiance. The sight was calculated to carry the minds of both back to the events of former years. But I noticed that Hall quickly changed the position of his chair, and sat down again with his back to the rising moon. He had managed to save some millions from the wreck of his vast fortune when artemisium started to go to the dogs, and I was now paying him one of my annual visits at his palatial home in California.

"Did I ever tell you of my last trip to the Teton?" he asked, as I continued to gaze contemplatively at the broad lunar disk which slowly detached itself from the horizon and began to swim in the clear evening sky.

"No," I replied, "but I should like to hear about it."

"Or of my last sight of Dr. Syx?"

"Indeed! I did not suppose that you ever saw him after

that conference in your mill, when he had to surrender half of the world to you."

"Once only I saw him again," said Hall, with a peculiar intonation.

"Pray go ahead, and tell me the whole story."

My friend lighted a fresh cigar, tipped his chair into a more comfortable position, and began:

"It was about seven years ago. I had long felt an unconquerable desire to have another look at the Teton and the scenes amid which so many strange events in my life had occurred. I thought of sending for you to go with me, but I knew you were abroad much of your time, and I could not be certain of catching you. Finally I decided to go alone. I travelled on horseback by way of the Snake River canyon, and arrived early one morning in Jackson's Hole. I can tell you it was a gloomy place, as barren and deserted as some of those Arabian wadies that you have been describing to me. The railroad had long ago been abandoned, and the site of the military camp could scarcely be recognized. An immense cavity with ragged walls showed where Dr. Syx's mill used to send up its plume of black smoke.

"As I stared up the gaunt form of the Teton, whose beetling precipices had been smashed and split by the great explosion, I was seized with a resistless impulse to climb it. I thought I should like to peer off again from that pinnacle which had once formed so fateful a watch-tower for me. Turning my horse loose to graze in the grassy river bottom, and carrying my rope tether along as a possible aid in climbing, I set out for the ascent. I knew I could not get up the precipices on the eastern side, which we were able to master with the aid of our balloon, and so I bore round, when I reached the steepest cliffs, until I was on the southwestern side of the peak, where the climbing was easier.

"But it took me a long time, and I did not reach the rift in the summit until just before sundown. Knowing that it would be impossible for me to descend at night, I bethought me of the enclosure of rocks, supposed to have been made by Indians, on the western pinnacle, and decided that I could pass the night there.

"The perpendicular buttress forming the easternmost and highest point of the Teton's head would have baffled me but for the fact that I found a long crack, probably an effect of the tremendous explosion, extending from bottom to top of the rock. Driving my toes and fingers into this rift, I managed, with a good deal of trouble, and no little peril, to reach the top. As I lifted myself over the edge and rose to my feet, imagine my amazement at seeing Dr. Syx standing within arm's-length of me!

"My breath seemed pent in my lungs, and I could not even utter the exclamation that rose to my lips. It was like meeting a ghost. Notwithstanding the many reports of his having been seen in various parts of the world, it had always been my conviction that he had perished in the explosion.

"Yet there he stood in the twilight, for the sun was hidden by the time I reached the summit, his tall form erect, and his black eyes gleaming under the heavy brows as he fixed them sternly upon my face. You know I never was given to losing my nerve, but I am afraid I lost it on that occasion. Again and again I strove to speak, but it was impossible to move my tongue. So powerless seemed my lungs that I wondered how I could continue breathing.

"The doctor remained silent, but his curious smile, which, as you know, was a thing of terror to most people, overspread his black-rimmed face and was broad enough to reveal the gleam of his teeth. I felt that he was looking me through and through. The sensation was as if he had transfixed me with an ice-cold blade. There was a gleam of devilish pleasure in his eyes, as though my evident suffering was a delight to him and a gratification of his vengeance. At length I succeeded in overcoming the feeling which oppressed me, and, making a step forward, I shouted in a strained voice,

"'You black Satan!'

"I cannot clearly explain the psychological process which led me to utter those words. I had never entertained any enmity towards Dr. Syx, although I had always regarded him as a heartless person, who had purposely led thousands to their ruin for his selfish gain, but I knew that he could not help hating me, and I felt now that, in some inexplicable manner, a struggle, not physical, but spiritual, was taking place between us, and my exclamation, uttered with surprising intensity, produced upon me, and apparently upon him, the effect of a desperate sword thrust which attains its mark.

"Immediately the doctor's form seemed to recede, as if he had passed the verge of the precipice behind him. At the same time it became dim, and then dimmer, until only the dark outlines, and particularly the jet-black eyes, glaring fiercely, remained visible. And still he receded, as though floating in the air, which was now silvered with the evening light, until he appeared to cross the immense atmospheric gulf over Jackson's Hole and paused on the rim of the horizon in the east.

"Then, suddenly, I became aware that the full moon had risen at the very place on the distant mountain-brow where the spectre rested, and as I continued to gaze, as if entranced, the face and figure of the doctor seemed slowly to frame themselves within the lunar disk, until at last he appeared to have quitted the air and the earth and to be frowning at me from the circle of the moon."

While Hall was pronouncing his closing words I had begun to stare at the moon with swiftly increasing interest, until, as his voice stopped, I exclaimed,

"Why, there he is now! Funny I never noticed it before. There's Dr. Syx's face in the moon, as plain as day."

"Yes," replied Hall, without turning round, "and I never like to look at it."

Choose from Thousands of 1stWorldLibrary Classics By

Adolphus WilliamWard
Aesop
Agatha Christie
Alexander Aaronsohn
Alexander Kielland
Alexandre Dumas
Alfred Gatty
Alfred Ollivant
Alice Duer Miller
Alice Turner Curtis
Alice Dunbar
Ambrose Bierce
Amelia E. Barr
Andrew Lang
Andrew McFarland Davis
Anna Sewell
Annie Besant
Annie Hamilton Donnell
Annie Payson Call
Anton Chekhov
Arnold Bennett
Arthur Conan Doyle
Arthur Ransome
Atticus
B. M. Bower
Basil King
Bayard Taylor
Ben Macomber
Booth Tarkington
Bram Stoker
C. Collodi
C. E. Orr
C. M. Ingleby
Carolyn Wells
Catherine Parr Traill
Charles A. Eastman
Charles Dickens
Charles Dudley Warner
Charles Farrar Browne
Charles Ives
Charles Kingsley
Charles Lathrop Pack
Charles Whibley
Charles Willing Beale
Charlotte M. Braeme
Charlotte M.Yonge
Clair W. Hayes
Clarence Day Jr.
Clarence E. Mulford

Clemence Housman
Confucius
Cornelis DeWitt Wilcox
Cyril Burleigh
D. H. Lawrence
Daniel Defoe
David Garnett
Don Carlos Janes
Donald Keyhole
Dorothy Kilner
Dougan Clark
E. Nesbit
E.P.Roe
E. Phillips Oppenheim
Edgar Allan Poe
Edgar Rice Burroughs
Edith Wharton
Edward J. O'Biren
John Cournos
Edwin L. Arnold
Eleanor Atkins
Elizabeth Cleghorn
Gaskell
Elizabeth Von Arnim
Ellem Key
Emily Dickinson
Erasmus W. Jones
Ernie Howard Pie
Ethel Turner
Ethel Watts Mumford
Eugenie Foa
Eugene Wood
Evelyn Everett-Green
Everard Cotes
F. J. Cross
Federick Austin Ogg
Ferdinand Ossendowski
Francis Bacon
Francis Darwin
Frances Hodgson Burnett
Frank Gee Patchin
Frank Harris
Frank Jewett Mather
Frank L. Packard
Frederick Trevor Hill
Frederick Winslow Taylor
Friedrich Kerst
Friedrich Nietzsche
Fyodor Dostoyevsky

Gabrielle E. Jackson
Garrett P. Serviss
Gaston Leroux
George Ade
Geroge Bernard Shaw
George Ebers
George Eliot
George MacDonald
George Orwell
George Tucker
George W. Cable
George Wharton James
Gertrude Atherton
Grace E. King
Grant Allen
Guillermo A. Sherwell
Gulielma Zollinger
Gustav Flaubert
H. A. Cody
H. B. Irving
H. G. Wells
H. H. Munro
H. Irving Hancock
H. Rider Haggard
H. W. C. Davis
Hamilton Wright Mabie
Hans Christian Andersen
Harold Avery
Harold McGrath
Harriet Beecher Stowe
Harry Houidini
Helent Hunt Jackson
Helen Nicolay
Hendy David Thoreau
Henrik Ibsen
Henry Adams
Henry Ford
Henry Frost
Henry James
Henry Jones Ford
Henry Seton Merriman
Henry Wadsworth
Longfellow
Henry W Longfellow
Herbert A. Giles
Herbert N. Casson
Herman Hesse
Homer
Honore De Balzac

Horace Walpole
Horatio Alger, Jr.
Howard Pyle
Howard R. Garis
Hugh Lofting
Hugh Walpole
Humphry Ward
Ian Maclaren
Israel Abrahams
J.G.Austin
J. Henri Fabre
J. M. Barrie
J. Macdonald Oxley
J. S. Knowles
J. Storer Clouston
Jack London
Jacob Abbott
James Allen
James Lane Allen
James Andrews
James Baldwin
James DeMille
James Joyce
James Oliver Curwood
James Oppenheim
James Otis
Jane Austen
Jens Peter Jacobsen
Jerome K. Jerome
John Burroughs
John F. Kennedy
John Gay
John Glasworthy
John Habberton
John Joy Bell
John Milton
John Philip Sousa
Jonathan Swift
Joseph Carey
Joseph Conrad
Joseph Jacobs
Julian Hawthrone
Julies Vernes
Justin Huntly McCarthy
Kakuzo Okakura
Kenneth Grahame
Kate Langley Bosher
L. A. Abbot
L. T. Meade
L. Frank Baum
Laura Lee Hope

Laurence Housman
Leo Tolstoy
Leonid Andreyev
Lewis Carroll
Lilian Bell
Lloyd Osbourne
Louis Tracy
Louisa May Alcott
Lucy Fitch Perkins
Lucy Maud Montgomery
Lydia Miller Middleton
Lyndon Orr
M. H. Adams
Margaret E. Sangster
Margaret Vandercook
Maria Edgeworth
Maria Thompson Daviess
Mariano Azuela
Marion Polk Angellotti
Mark Overton
Mark Twain
Mary Austin
Mary Cole
Mary Rowlandson
Mary Wollstonecraft
Shelley
Max Beerbohm
Myra Kelly
Nathaniel Hawthrone
O. F. Walton
Oscar Wilde
Owen Johnson
P.G.Wodehouse
Paul and Mable Thorn
Paul G. Tomlinson
Paul Severing
Peter B. Kyne
Plato
R. Derby Holmes
R. L. Stevenson
Rabindranath Tagore
Rahul Alvares
Ralph Waldo Emmerson
Rene Descartes
Rex E. Beach
Richard Harding Davis
Richard Jefferies
Robert Barr
Robert Frost
Robert Gordon Anderson
Robert L. Drake

Robert Lansing
Robert Michael Ballantyne
Robert W. Chambers
Rosa Nouchette Carey
Ross Kay
Rudyard Kipling
Samuel B. Allison
Samuel Hopkins Adams
Sarah Bernhardt
Selma Lagerlof
Sherwood Anderson
Sigmund Freud
Standish O'Grady
Stanley Weyman
Stella Benson
Stephen Crane
Stewart Edward White
Stijn Streuvels
Swami Abhedananda
Swami Parmananda
T. S. Ackland
The Princess Der Ling
Thomas A. Janvier
Thomas A Kempis
Thomas Anderton
Thomas Bailey Aldrich
Thomas Bulfinch
Thomas De Quincey
Thomas H. Huxley
Thomas Hardy
Thomas More
Thornton W. Burgess
U. S. Grant
Valentine Williams
Victor Appleton
Virginia Woolf
Walter Scott
Washington Irving
Wilbur Lawton
Wilkie Collins
Willa Cather
Willard F. Baker
William Makepeace
Thackeray
William W. Walter
Winston Churchill
Yei Theodora Ozaki
Young E. Allison
Zane Grey